OLIVIA JONES

PHILLIP A. BROWN

OLIVIA JONES

PHILLIP A. BROWN

GATEWAY
EDUCATIONAL
FOUNDATION & INSTITUTE
They had a dream...

Lancaster, California

in association with

Night Star Publisher
San Diego, California

GATEWAY EDUCATIONAL FOUNDATION & INSTITUTE
Lancaster, California
gatewayeducationalfoundationandinstitute.org
oliviajonesjourney.com
info@oliviajonesjourney.com

in association with
NIGHT STAR PUBLISHER
San Diego, California
Printed in the United States

First Edition
ISBN: 978-1-0880-0186-8 (print)
ISBN: 978-1-0880-0178-3 (ebook)

Editing and Book Design
Jan Carpenter Tucker • nightstarpublisher.com

Cover and Frontispiece Illustration and Design
Wendell Wiggins

Production Notes
Fonts used for print book:
ITC Stone Informal (Olivia's voice and general information)
and ITC Stone Sans (narrator's voice)
P22 Vincent (graphic embellishment)

CONTENTS

Special Dedication • 7

Dedications • 8

Acknowledgments • 10

Foreword • 16

Reflection • 18

Historical Information • 21

Epilogue • 23

Prologue • 25

The Journey

Greene County, Alabama • 28

Dallas County, Alabama • 31

Mobile, Alabama • 77

Bibliography • 147

Glossary of Legal Terms • 150

Advance Reviews • 152

About the Author • 157

About the Cover Artist • 159

About 1965 • 160

SPECIAL DEDICATION

This book is dedicated to the men and women who gave the ultimate sacrifice for the freedom of the American Negro—their lives! I hope this generation and those to come will keep these American heroes alive in their hearts and minds. We could never repay them for what they gave us.

Medgar Evers
(38 years old)
James Chaney
(21 years old)
Andrew Goodman
(20 years old)
Michael Schwerner
(25 years old)
Jimmy Lee Jackson
(26 years old)
Minister James Reeb
(38 years old)
Viola Gregg Liuzzo
(39 years old)

DEDICATION

In memory of my mother

Trennie Wright-Brown Grau

Thank you for being my number one fan always! You've always believed in me even when I had no clue! And you trusted me so much. At nineteen years old you trusted that I could drive from Berkeley, California to San Diego, pick up your precious granddaughter, Tracey (four years old), and drive her to her mom (Jaki) cross country to New York City. That journey and move to NYC helped me to become a man. I found my strength, focus and a new direction which put me closer in harmony with myself. But even before that journey, you had the foresight to send me to Albany, California to live with Aunt Arlene (my second mom) when I was a bit out of control as a teenager. You always knew and acted on that spirit on my behalf. I'm laughing, thinking about how you became a tennis enthusiast in support of my love and involvement in the sport. You called me to give the latest news on Venus and Serena Williams...and how upset at them you would be when they would lose a set or, God forbid, a match! I miss you so much!

DEDICATION

To my children

Randy Wonzur Ratcliff
Bryan Anthony Brown
Chauntelle Evon Ratcliff
Gabrielle Ratcliff-Henderson
Devyn Elisabeth Brown
Jazmyn Brown-Osman
Erica Denise Calloway

I love you. You inspire me to always strive hard to make the playing field for you just a little bit fairer. I'm in awe of how you soar with the smallest amount of wind beneath your wings! I believe and trust that you and your children are the generations that our ancestors hoped and dreamed for. So, this is your season. Go and bring forth a harvest for the beloved community!

ACKNOWLEDGMENTS

To the Black men, women and children of Selma, Alabama who personally sacrificed so much during one of the most perilous times in our American history, I dedicate this story—which is really your story—of a collective struggle and journey to "make America fair for all people." You are truly American heroes, and we all owe you a debt we can never repay. Thank you!

To my dad, James "Jim" Brown, you gave me a vision of what it is to live a life that betters the lives of the people in your community. Thank you for passing the torch on to me. Your and Genise's legacy and vision for Gateway Educational Foundation and its work will live on to engage future generations of young people in the importance of Selma, and the history it holds. You charted a path for me which holds great promise for our collective future.

To my bride, Lisa Deleon Ratcliff Brown, your support, encouragement and push have made me a better man, father, papa and husband. Thank you for believing in my ability to write this little girl's story. And to our grandchildren, Elijah and Elise Henderson, your excitement in hearing me read "Olivia's" journey, and desire to hear more as it was unfolding in my writings, really pushed me to become a writer. I love you both so much!

A special dedication to Rev. Dr. C. T. Vivian, Mayor James Perkins, Jr., Professor Bernard Lafayette, Dr. Clarence B. Jones, Ambassador Andrew J. Young, Jr. and Amelia Boynton Robinson (who passed two months prior to my first visit to Selma). It is your writings on Selma's voting rights history you lived, and the personal stories from that history that you graciously shared with me, that's the fuel for my writing "Olivia Jones's" journey. Thank you for making America a bit more fair for all. Thank you for your friendship!

I believe the ingredients for every successful journey includes family, friends, a team and a previously unknown equation—The Village! My big sister, Jaki Brown, you have been an amazing source for encouragement and leadership in forging important relationships for this journey. And when you called me from Aunt Arlene's with excitement after finally reading the draft manuscript, that made my world spin in possibilities! Thank you so much!

Our daughter, Twylah Lacroix Ratcliff, you are my Barnabas—you epitomize encouragement. From the first read as I was writing "Olivia's" journey you have been a sounding-board of inspiration—thank you!

Rory Pullens, I'm not sure where to begin... encouragement, sounding board, support (financially and otherwise). You've graciously opened your Rolodex to me as I've journeyed to pass the torch from this

American history to our youth and young adults. You've trusted and believed from the start. And as a result, Gateway Educational Foundation and Institute and I have an amazing partnership and relationship with both Skirball Cultural Center and the Museum of African American Art. Thank you!

Speaking of: Thank you, Jessie Kornberg and Berlinda "Auntie Ber" Fontenot-Jamerson, respectively. You're both amazing! Jessie, from our first conversation to your masterful facilitation of the "Passing the Torch" conversation with Mayor Perkins, Professor Lafayette and Ambassador Young, you have been a supporter. And now, as president and CEO of Skirball you've embraced the "Olivia Jones" book launch in such a powerful move—as host and partner! And with such a dynamic Skirball Team (Sheri, Jen, Marlene and Isabel)... Wow, again thank you so much! Auntie Ber, you have welcomed my calls—day, night and weekend—without hesitation, and have provided mentorship, friendship, your wealth of knowledge and expertise and relationships to encourage me. And you have supported me through strategic relationships and sponsors you've invited into my journey. Through your leadership the Museum of African American Art so graciously hosted our "Passing the Torch" event for the community and Los Angeles Unified School District high school students. It was a watershed moment—thank you!

Deboraha and Steward Townson, I wish that everyone could have friends like you! Thank you for always saying yes—to hosting Mayor James Perkins, Jr., Mayor Henry Hearns and Professor Bernard Lafayette. But also, for hosting our first "Olivia Jones" pre-launch celebration event on Juneteenth at your beautiful home and ranch—my home away from home!

Connie and Yellow Slaughter, you two are amazing friends. Thank you for hosting that great meal for our civil/voting rights icons; it left an indelible impression. They now have a fondness for the AV!

Arena Cole, you are such an amazing spirit—the energy in the room shifts to a higher vibration when you enter! Thank you for opening your home to host our second "Olivia Jones" pre-launch event. The intimacy provided conversations steeped in the richness of our African American legacy and history. It helped to validate for me what I hoped to be true—that "Olivia's" journey would facilitate that kind of discourse around our history.

Sharon Rosenthal, thank you for the many conversations we've had while you were providing the first edits to the "Olivia Jones" manuscript. Those conversations helped illuminate new possibilities in sharing "Olivia's" story, beyond a traditional retail audience to—maybe—an educational and school audience. Your belief in her story to educate young people gave me a higher level of confidence.

Amaya Hawkins, Lauren Michelle Hardge, Courtney Comer—you three are awesome young ladies! "Olivia" would be proud to have you as big sisters. Thank you for bringing your gifts and talents to help illuminate her story and for believing in the work of "Passing the Torch!"

Rain Wilson, my Sista, you are an incredibly spiritually-gifted messenger from God. He put you in my path more than a decade ago and in such a natural, fortuitous, on-purpose encounter, and in a way that only He could—which led to you inviting me to an amazing play ("Jungle Kings") that you wrote, casted and directed. You have gifted me and Gateway Educational Foundation and Institute your "Star" and shone it brightly illuminating the work of "Passing the Torch to America's Youth." Now you are doing the same for "Olivia Jones!" Thank you for not only believing in me and the work of Gateway, but for sacrificing your time, talents and gifts on our behalf. I love you so much, little sister! Believe me now—this is our season to reap the harvest from what we've sown!

Christine Swanson—that unknown equation for me—you have elevated the spirit of "Olivia Jones's" story with your reflection and story synopsis to a place I could not have imagined prior. I am so very honored to have you as part of "Olivia's" journey and I am also so thankful to big sis, Jaki Brown, for believing enough in the draft manuscript to put it in your hands. Thank you for believing!

To all the early readers of my manuscript I'm not going to try and list your names, but you and I know who you are—THANK YOU SO MUCH! Being validated for a creative work is like water to a duck—it is so very necessary, and you've helped to provide that for me, and I thank you from the bottom of my heart!

Jan Carpenter Tucker, my editor and co-publisher, thank you for bringing your amazing talents to this project. You've known me, my character and nature, well over four decades and it shows in the care that you've taken in helping me put "Olivia's" story in book form. You've made it all real! Thank you—you're making me a better author.

Phillip A. Brown

FOREWORD

History is such a powerful tool to have on one's toolbelt as you journey through this life. Having been a student of and a participant in making history, I can tell you that my dear friend and author, Phil Brown, has proven time and again to demonstrate his sincere reverence for history, and passing forward the legacies of those African American men and women who've sacrificed so much in challenging America to live up to its founding principles.

We can all debate which platforms are best for engaging current and future generations of young people with American history. But what I don't believe is up for debate is the masterful way the author, Phil Brown, tells this fictional journey of Olivia Jones, with real lived history woven throughout. It reads as compelling as any autobiography tale. After reading the draft manuscript I called Phil to question him: "Is this her true story?" Mind you, he told me it was a fictional story prior to sending the draft over. The story was so captivating that I completely lost myself in the pages. This story will capture the attention and the imagination of its reader—as it did me and my wife, Kate, my partner of 53 years. "Once you start reading her story, you can't put it down!"

Both Kate and I are educators, so we know firsthand

the power of being able to engage students and young adults—once you have their attention you can teach them anything—including history! Olivia Jones will grab their attention while simultaneously teaching them lessons of struggle in our American history. Young people typically get stories of history told through the lens of much older adults. This story is refreshing as it's told through the lens of an eleven-year-old little girl. This story has the potential to inspire its readers to seek out other stories rooted in the history of the civil rights era. Kate and I are proud of Phil for writing this great story—and we highly recommend this book for young people—but also, our personal observation and enjoyment of this story tells us that adults of all ages will enjoy this journey, and the history it weaves in and out of...A must read!

Professor Bernard & Kate Lafayette

Professor Bernard Lafayette, Jr., (born July 29, 1940) is a longtime civil rights activist and organizer, who was a leader in the civil rights movement. He played a leading role in early organizing of the Selma voting rights movement; was a member of the Nashville student movement; and worked closely throughout the 1960s movements with groups such as the Student Nonviolent Coordinating Committee (SNCC), and the Southern Christian Leadership Conference (SCLC).

REFLECTION

This young character, "Olivia Jones," breathes in the spirit of Amelia Boynton, the mother of the Selma voting rights movement. I knew Amelia for well over 50 years. I didn't know her during her youth. But I imagine her much like "Olivia Jones"—in that they both showed a tremendous heart and passion, put into action, for the well-being of others. At 10 years old Amelia was helping her mother get out the white women vote in her hometown, Savannah, Georgia. She had a spirit that carried her all the way through President Obama's 2012 campaign—where she helped to get out the vote at 101 years old. Reading the compelling journey of "Olivia Jones," I couldn't help but think of the indomitable spirit of Amelia Boynton. I believe this story is right for these times. Young people are searching for their voice—their power!

Phil Brown has written a most compelling story that gives honor to Alabama's rich civil and voting rights history. But it's only fitting in that Phil and his wife, Lisa, have taken the baton passed to them from his dad, my friend, Jim Brown, who was engaged in the voting rights struggle with us. And who started a nonprofit corporation to pass the torch of that history to America's youth.

We have a generation or two—through no fault

of their own—that know very little, if anything, of Alabama's civil and voting rights history of the 1950s and '60s. That means we have a collective duty to find and use every means available to share those stories of history—even through historical fictions like "Olivia Jones." Many lessons can be learned through her story.

I know the importance of history as a guidepost for contemporary society's struggle for human rights—I know because I've been there in this struggle to help make our society just. Reading the "Olivia Jones" story and journeying back through time—people and places in history—was a true joy! And I have no doubt that anyone reading this book—young or old—will enjoy her journey as well! My young friend and author, Phil Brown, does us all proud...and I know his dad would be proud as well.

Ambassador Andrew J. Young, Jr.

HISTORICAL INFORMATION

Characters and Places
(mentioned in this book)

- *Thurgood Marshall (Supreme Court Justice, served 1967–1991)*

- *Jimmy Lee Jackson (his death in 1965 led to the Selma to Montgomery marches)*

- *Dr. Martin Luther King, Jr.*

- *Rev. Thomas E. Gilmore (first elected Black sheriff of Greene County; the "Sheriff Without a Gun")*

- *James Joseph Reeb was an American Unitarian Universalist minister, pastor and activist killed during the voting rights movement in Selma, Alabama, March 11, 1965*

- *Brown Chapel African Methodist Episcopal (A.M.E.) Church*

- *Dexter Avenue Baptist Church*

- *Selma, Alabama*

- *Edmund Pettus Bridge*

- *George Wallace (Governor of Alabama, 1963–1987)*

- *Samuel and Amelia Boynton Home, an Alabama Historic site—1315 Lapsley Street (now 1315 Boyntons Street)*

EPILOGUE

Virginia, Thomas and Jimmy walked down the steps of the United States Supreme Court. Olivia:

Mama say when Supreme Court Justice Mr. Marshall spoke, it was like the heavens opened up an' the power of God filled the courtroom. Mama was there but she didn't remember what exactly he say. After he spoke, an' they announced the vote, people was just overjoyed an' some people even cried. She say it was then—at that moment—Daddy had his freedom! He an' Mama left Washington, DC, an' come back home to Eutaw, Alabama. You know, Mama used to always say, one day America would be fair for all people. I think for Mama, that day finally come to be true!

THE END...

One more thing: Mama went back to school so she could become a lawyer someday, just like that Supreme Court Justice, Mr. Thurgood Marshall, so she could help America to be fair for more people.

PROLOGUE

I'm Oli [pronounced Ah-lee'] an' I'm somewhat of a tomboy. Most people think Oli is short for Olivia but it's not. I don't know how I learned it, but I can fight, real good, an' I'm stronger than most of the boys around here. Some say I move real fast like Muhammad Ali. I'm smart an' I always win, so that's why they call me Oli.

My best friend—maybe my only friend—is Mo. Well, his real name is Bartholomew. I use to tease him an' call him MEOW, like a cat. He'd get all mad 'cause he didn't like cats. He was kinda scared of 'em—especially after that stupid boy Tommy played that Halloween trick on Mo by throw'n that black cat on his back.

It's always Mo, me an' Champ, Mo's German Shepherd dog. Champ even sleeps with Mo—every night! Me an' Mo, we kinda like twins, except he a boy an' we got different moms an' dads. But we was both born on the same day of the month, six months apart. I was born on April fifth, 1968 an' Mo was born on October fifth, 1967.

Mama was real sad on the day I was born 'cause Dr. Martin Luther King, Jr. was killed on the day before I come into the world. An' my daddy was over in Vietnam fight'n in the war that Dr. King was against. Mama say Daddy didn't even know I was be'n born—at least she didn't think so. (Daddy didn't know mama was pregnant when he left for the army 'cause Mama didn't know either.)

Mama didn't have no letters from Daddy an' she didn't know if he received her letters tell'n him 'bout me. Daddy didn't even know my name when I was be'n born, so Mama was really sad on that day.

See, another reason me an' Mo like twins 'cause our daddies was best friends—just like me an' Mo is. Mama tell'n me they was always together. Mo's daddy an' my daddy got taken in the Army together, too.

One time I remember I heard Mama talk'n to Uncle Wayne—I was 'bout five or six years old—an' Mama was say'n how the Vietnam War was either kill'n or change'n all the Black men that was over there. She say, like Mo's daddy, Mr. Wright. Mama say, when he was in the Vietnam War he lost his left arm fight'n over there. She say when he come home from that Vietnam War, he was angry an' real mean—always drink'n an' fight'n with Mo's mama. Then one day he just left!

Mo don't remember him though—'cause he was only 'bout two years old or younger—so he don't know his dad neither.

I have a picture with all of us together—well kinda. Mama had this picture that I taken from her drawer. It was Mama, Daddy, Mo's mama an' daddy. An' Mo's mama was soon fat 'cause she was pregnant in the picture with Mo in her belly. I say, "Mama, she look like she gonna have that baby right then." But Mama laughed—an' say she was only seven months pregnant. Mama say she found out three weeks later that she was pregnant, too—with me inside her belly—but Daddy was already gone to Vietnam. So we was kinda all there together, but you just couldn't see everybody—like me an' Mo. I keeps that picture with me wherever I go.

Mama say I'm a lot like my daddy 'cause I'm always fix'n on things like bikes an' figure'n stuff out. Like that one time when Mo an' me was fish'n on the lake with Uncle Wayne in his boat, an' the motor just stopped runn'n. Uncle Wayne didn't know what to do—so I started look'n at the motor an' I see where the gas wasn't go'n to the motor. So I pulled the hose loose an' cleaned it an' the motor started runn'n again. Uncle Wayne just shook his head an' say, "You just like your daddy, an' he could fix anything!"

I'm pretty smart in school, too—well I like math a lot—but I really don't like school that much. Sometimes I just didn't go. But when I did I get good grades.

I do have another friend—well kinda. His name is Jimmy—well his real name is James Robert Lee, Jr.—but he don't like that name 'cause he don't like his daddy much. Jimmy is grown though—like maybe twenty-five or even thirty years old—he is grown! When I didn't go to school, I would ride my bike over to the lake an' Jimmy would be there, sitt'n in his big-o-car—he say it's a classic—1959 Oldsmobile ninety-eight. It was just a big-o-car to me.

Jimmy an' me would just be talk'n—you know 'bout things we liked, like fish'n an' travel'n—well I ain't never been nowhere except here in this town. But when Jimmy be talk'n 'bout all the places he been, I thought I really like to go there, too, one day. He likes math, too, an' he helped me with my math. He showed me how to understand it, way easier than my teacher at school. Jimmy is really smart. But he say it wasn't always easy for him when he was in school. He say that he had someone to help him, too.

THE JOURNEY

Greene County, Alabama

Champ's always bark'n at Jimmy—when Mo would come with me to the lake—so Jimmy didn't like it too much when Mo would come with me 'cause Champ wouldn't stop bark'n at him. I remember this one time though, me, Mo an' Champ was all sitt'n in Jimmy's big-o-car an' he was talk'n 'bout travel'n to far places like India an' Ghana, when he was live'n in Boston an' go'n to school there. He traveled do'n missionary work with other students. Suddenly me an' Mo, we had the same question—at the same time—we ask Jimmy, "Why you didn't go over to Vietnam, like our daddies did?"

Jimmy just stared out the window at the lake—he didn't say another word. Funny thing though, Champ sat there the whole time, just stare'n at Jimmy stare'n out at the lake. After 'bout five or ten minutes (it seem like an hour) Mo an' me opened the door an' got out the car. Champ was still sitt'n there stare'n at Jimmy, so we had to call Champ—then he come. I never told Mo, but when I looked at Jimmy's face as we was gett'n out the car, there was a tear runn'n down Jimmy's face. Well, me an' Mo, we never talked 'bout go'n to Vietnam again around Jimmy.

Downtown Eutaw, 1979

At least once a week Mo an' me would ride our bikes into town—to the Eutaw sheriff's office—an' ask the sheriff the same questions 'bout Mo's daddy. We been try'n to find our daddies as long as I can remember. But when we got old enough to be gone all day without Mama come look'n for us, we start come'n there, an' ask'n 'bout our daddies.

When I first told Mama that me an' Mo went to the sheriff's office in town to try an' find my daddy, Mama looked at me real serious an' she told me never to go down to the sheriff's office ask'n 'bout my daddy again. She say it would just be better for daddy if I didn't do that again. I didn't understand, but Mama was so serious! When I told Mo what Mama was say'n, he just say, "well, she didn't say you can't come there with me, look'n for my daddy." So we figured, if we find Mo's daddy, we would find my daddy, too—'cause they was always together, like me an' Mo.

This one day though, Sheriff Gilmore had some good news for Mo an' me. He say he had found some information out 'bout Mo's daddy. It turned out that Mr. Wright had filled out some papers for Army medical benefits as a fully disabled veteran (from agent orange exposure an' loss of limb) an' he listed an address in Dallas County as his home.

Mo an' me was so excited when we hear the news, that we went runn'n out the sheriff's office! We had forgot to let Champ out the door, an' we even forgot 'bout gett'n our bikes. We was just runn'n—then we stopped. When we come back to get Champ an' our bikes, we asked Sheriff Gilmore, "Where is Dallas County? Is that in America?" He laughed, then he told us it was right here in the state of Alabama, 'bout sixty miles away from Eutaw, or 'bout an hour drive by car.

Me an' Mo started make'n plans while we was ride'n our bikes back home from Eutaw. We say that next Saturday we would ride our bikes to Dallas County where Sheriff Gilmore say Mo's daddy live. But I know we was gonna need Jimmy's help to figure out just where Dallas County was, an' a map on how to get there by ride'n our bikes.

Dallas County, Alabama

Mr. Wright had finally received the medical treatment and disability benefits he needed to stabilize his life. He had met a girl in Birmingham—after he divorced Mo's mama. They married and settled in her hometown of Selma, Alabama where they started a new family. They had two little girls.

Downtown Eutaw, 1970

Oli's daddy got out of the army in October 1970. Although he was coming home a war hero, having been awarded the Medal of Honor, he had struggled with all of what he saw and did as a soldier in Vietnam, just to survive. Coming home was a mix of emotions for him—sadness, joy and apprehension—after being gone for so long, with no contact or communication with his wife, Virginia. Would Virginia welcome him home? Would she be angry at him? Could she ever forgive him?

As Thomas arrived in town, he found himself passing in front of the American Southern Baptist Congregational Church. A rage began to build within him. Just beyond the church was the pastoral parsonage, the house where Pastor Reverend James Robert Lee, Sr. resided.

Thomas has a flashback—Vietnam

Thomas is in an ambush battle that he and his fellow troops are engaged in. The men are under heavy gunfire—fighting against the Vietcong. A grenade explodes killing some of the soldiers and wounding others, including Wally Wright (Mo's daddy).

Thomas has another flash back—
Greene County, 1963

Thomas is in the backwoods where he's a fourteen-year-old teen. He and another boy are horse-playing when they stumble upon a gathering—a large group of men—all wearing white robes and white hoods. It is a lynching. Thomas and the other boy are now hiding in the bushes. They are witness to a mob of hooded Klansmen lynching a young Black boy about their age.

Thomas's vision fades back
to the present moment

Thomas entered the side door to the parsonage. Within moments inside, he encountered Pastor Lee. With a rage in his spirit, Thomas pointed his finger at Pastor Lee and said, "I know everything you did to that boy from Dallas County. You're no preacher—man of God—you're a Ku Klux Klan devil hating murderer!"

"Get out of my house you nigger bastard," hissed Pastor Lee. "Do you think anybody is gonna believe a damn thing that come out of your nigga mouth about me boy? I'm the closest thing to God that your black ass will ever see!"

Thomas, his chest pounding with adrenalin, "I wasn't the only one to see what you did to that boy. Jimmy was there, too. He saw you murder that boy. Your son knows you the devil!"

Thomas turned to leave, just as Pastor Lee swung the fireplace iron, hitting Thomas across the left side of his head. It glanced off into his shoulder. Thomas stumbled forward against the door. Catching his balance, he stood facing Pastor Lee, blood running down his face. As Pastor Lee swung the iron again, Thomas caught it with his left hand, grabbed the pastor by the throat with his right hand, and raised him up off the floor. Pastor Lee struggled a bit— then his body went limp. He was…dead?

He and Wally are walking through the woods on a dirt road headed to school. Wally asks Thomas, "Did you hear about what happened the other night to that boy, Tony? The boy who played baseball against us—you know the one." Thomas stops walking, reaches up with his hands, covers his ears and starts yelling at Wally, "I don't wanna hear about that. I don't wanna hear no more!" Then he grabs Wally by the collar, lifting him off the ground. Wally is shocked and scared—really frightened—at what is happening.

Suddenly Thomas lets go of Wally. He starts to run, and run, and run—faster and faster—for about a quarter mile. He stops, tears rolling down his face. Thomas falls to his knees and screams at the top of his voice, "God, why? Why they do that to that boy? Why did you make me see that, Lord? Why, Lord? Why they do that?"

Thomas and Wally never again spoke of that day nor of Tony, the boy lynched by the Klan that night.

Downtown Eutaw, 1970
(at the Parsonage)

Thomas realized what he had just done, with Pastor Lee lying there on the floor. He hurried out of the side door, grabbing his duffel bag that he had left on the side porch.

He tossed it over his shoulder and started to run through the back of the property into the woods behind the parsonage. He headed toward the address he had for Virginia's home, about five miles south of Eutaw. But what Thomas didn't realize, until he stopped running (about two miles outside of town), was that he had left a piece of evidence in the pastor's home.

As he looked back over his right shoulder to see if anyone was following him, he saw that the Army patch on the jacket shoulder was torn off. He quickly realized that it must have happened at the parsonage when the pastor was trying to get free of Thomas's grip. He now knew that they would be after him—or at the least, they would be after an Army soldier with a tear on his uniform.

As Thomas began running again, he started having second thoughts about going to Virginia's home. They could track him there, and she would be in danger, too. But where else could he go now? He had finally felt that he was ready and could come back home to his wife, Virginia. He had hoped to continue his mental healing from the emotional scars of the Vietnam War. Coming back home— there in Eutaw with Virginia—could be a safe place to live while figuring out his life and repairing his marriage. But now, it only felt like a faraway dream.

In the distance—breaking his thoughts—he could hear the sound of a siren blaring in the night. He quickened his pace, deciding to continue on to Virginia's home.

Pastor Lee's wife made her way down the stairs, after the house fell silent for a little while. She had heard the rumbling a bit earlier; however, thinking Pastor was moving a chair or something across the floor, she was not concerned. She had thought maybe she heard some voices, but figured it must have been the radio, because Pastor always had it going.

She screamed as she quickened her steps toward her husband's body lying on the floor. Believing Pastor had fallen—stricken from a heart attack—she quickly grabbed the phone and dialed 911 emergency.

As Thomas made his way through the woods, his thoughts kept racing through his head. *Why did I wait so long to come home? Why didn't I write Virginia to say I was coming home? Does she still love me?* And now this thing he just did. He was sure he left that preacher dead.

Virginia's home sat on a large parcel (one and a half acres) of land on the edge of the rural community of Eutaw (about three-hundred residents). On her property there were many large cedar pine trees scattered, with clearings dispersed about the property.

When Thomas arrived at Virginia's property, the sky was clear and moonlit. It was around nine-thirty on a cool fall night in October. Thomas found himself hiding beside a large cedar pine tree to the rear of the house, where lights were shining through several windows out into the night. He watched a silhouetted figure moving through the house until a woman appeared in the window. It was Virginia, taking a seat in a chair in a bedroom.

As Thomas stared at her sitting there, the emotions began welling up within him. He began to cry softly, thinking about how much he loved her, and now missed her touch, and being there with her...feeling like he had been a coward, for letting all this time pass and not writing or coming home sooner. And for staying on base while on his leave, prior to his second deployment to Vietnam. Thomas knew right then that even in his brokenness, from the mental and physical scars of the Vietnam War, the woman he left back home would have loved him through it all.

Thomas was quickly brought back to his current situation when he heard sounds in the distance, in the direction that he had just traveled. Reaching into his duffel bag, Thomas pulled out a small Army green metal box and a large Army knife. He began clearing leaves and fallen bark on the ground from around the base of the tree, then started digging a hole big enough to bury the metal box. He was careful to brush the leaves and bark back over the spot where the box was buried.

Looking up at Virginia one last time as she sat there in the window, Thomas knew he'd never see her again. How could he? Would he even survive the night?

As Thomas rose up and turned away to run back toward the woods to evade being captured—just as his eyes were no longer focused on the window where Virginia was sitting—a little girl's image appeared in the window. She was holding a large book in her hand, extending it out to Virginia. Then she climbed into Virginia's lap. Thomas had already disappeared back into the woods.

Greene County, 1979

It was late when me an' Mo got home from the sheriff's office with the news 'bout Mo's daddy. Mo asked me if I had my lucky necklace on. I say yep, an' I pulled the chain up from my shirt an' showed him the tag that had my daddy's name an' a lot of numbers on it.

Oli's flashback—Greene County, 1973

Mo an' me was at my house celebrate'n my five-year-old birthday. We was play'n in my backyard. Uncle Wayne had give me some garden tools an' some seeds for my birthday.

Me an' Mo was out in the backyard digg'n by that big-o pine tree to plant the flower seeds, an' while we was digg'n, we found a green metal box. We run into the house an' told Mama we found a treasure box! It was all rusty, so it was hard to open.

When Mama cleaned it off an' opened it, that's when she find this chain an' a bunch of unopened letters from Mama to Daddy an' a medal with a ribbon (Medal of Honor) attached to it. Mama just started cry'n when she see what was inside. Mama had been pray'n to God 'bout my daddy. Mama say it was an answer to her prayers.

I didn't understand then, but Mama knew my daddy had placed that green box there by that tree. Mama put the necklace over my head an' around my neck an' she say, "This belong to your daddy. When you wear it, your daddy is always right here with you babe, right here next to your heart."

**Oli's flashback fades back
to the present moment**

Mo an' me agreed to go to the lake after Sunday school tomorrow, skipp'n church service so we could find Jimmy. Mama always stayed after church service help'n the Pastor an' the ushers clean'n up after the service. That gave me an' Mo time to go see Jimmy at the lake an' then get home before Mama for supper.

When morn'n come, I told Mama I was gonna

ride my bike to Sunday school instead of walk'n with her. Mama didn't see the backpack I had taken with me so I could carry my tennis shoes, jeans an' jacket. Mo rode his bike, too—an' yep, Mo brought Champ to Sunday school, too. As soon as Sunday school was over, I changed into the clothes in my backpack, an' then we took off for the lake to find Jimmy. Mama say she was gonna be late come'n home 'cause she was help'n Pastor Winewright get ready for a big church conference next weekend in Atlanta.

Mo didn't have to worry 'bout his Mama, Ms. Rosie Mae, find'n out that he skipped church service, 'cause Mama say she stopped go'n to church most of the time, after Mo's daddy left home. Mama say Ms. Rosie Mae use to sing in the choir with her. Rosie Mae had an outgo'n personality, she was loose, fast an' fun to be around. She was also highly influenceable by whatever the current events of the day an' the people involved in them.

Oli tells what Mama said about Selma, Alabama, 1965

Mama say it was Ms. Rosie Mae, Mama an' Daddy that drove to a place called Selma, Alabama in 1965. It was the time Mama heard Dr. Martin Luther King, Jr. speak. They all went to a big church in Selma—Brown Chapel AME—where hundreds of people was all gathered to march with Dr. King to Montgomery, Alabama.

Mama say that Ms. Rosie Mae was so excited to be there in Selma with Dr. King that she just upped an' left Mama an' Daddy so she could push through the crowd to get closer to Dr. King at the front of the march.

Funny thing though—Mama say that while they was march'n an' look'n for Ms. Rosie Mae, the marchers stopped on a bridge over the Alabama River. They all kneeled down an' prayed, got back up, turned around an' marched back to the church where they started from.

Mama say they was a little confused at why they stopped the march an' come back. But she was kinda happy 'cause she could only march that one day. Montgomery was a long ways to walk, 'bout fifty or sixty miles, an' Mama had to be back home before the next morn'n ready for school. Mama always wanted to go to college when she was in high school, so school'n was very important to Mama.

The funny thing was, when Mama an' daddy finally caught up with Ms. Rosie Mae, she was with Mo's daddy, Wally Wright. Mo's daddy had went to the march with his granddaddy earlier that morn'n. Mama say that Ms. Rosie Mae knew Wally from school but after that day, Ms. Rosie Mae started really like'n Wally. She thought he was so brave to be in the march with Dr. King, but Mama say also, it was 'cause Wally's granddaddy was friends with Dr. King. An' Ms. Rosie Mae got to meet Dr. King that day dur'n the march

41

'cause of Mo's daddy. She was impressed. After that, that's
when Ms. Rosie Mae started date'n Mo's daddy.

Her an' Mama was just sixteen years old when they
marched with Dr. King that day. Mama say she found out
later on, that a White minister name James Reeb, that
marched with them on the bridge that day, was lynched by a
group of angry White men who didn't want Black people to be
free, an' have the right to vote. An' that angry White people
didn't want other White people to help Blacks to be free an'
have the vote. Mama say the reason Dr. King was march'n
to Montgomery was 'cause a Black man name Jimmy Lee
Jackson who fought in the Vietnam War was killed 'cause he
wanted to vote.

Oli's back to the present moment

There was Jimmy's car, right where he always be
parked. Mo was so excited when we got in the car to
tell Jimmy 'bout Mo's daddy, that Mo couldn't breathe.
Mo started gasp'n for air really bad. Jimmy jumped out
the car an' come around to Mo's side in the back seat.
He got Mo out an' sit him down on the ground. He told
Mo to hold his hands up high an' try to relax by look'n
at the water move'n calmly across the lake. "Breathe
slowly," he told Mo—an' Mo finally started to breath'n
better. Mo had bronchial asthma when he was a baby,
but by the time he started second grade—'round six or

seven years old—he didn't get sick no more. Mo was really scared after he started breath'n good, wonder'n if his asthma had come back.

Jimmy helped Mo an' me figure out how to go to Dallas County to find Mo's daddy's house. Jimmy pulled a big map of Alabama out his glove box. He showed us where we was—there at the lake—an' where Dallas County was on the map. He circled the town call Selma on the map. I got so excited 'cause I remembered, that's where Mama an' Daddy marched with Dr. King! I told Mo all 'bout it later.

Jimmy say he will find out on Monday what bus go from Eutaw to Selma, an' he would get a schedule for us, an' that he would give us the money for two round trip tickets. Mo an' me was so excited ride'n our bikes back home that Mo was cough'n all the way. We stopped two or three times so he could catch his breath. But we was just so excited that we was go'n to find Mo's daddy on Saturday!

On Monday I was still excited all day, but I didn't see Mo at school at all. So after school I rode my bike to Mo's house. Mo's mama answered the door. She say Mo was sick, an' that his asthma come back. She say he was rest'n—the doctor give him some medicine to rest—an'

that he was asleep.

Mo was sick on Tuesday an' on Wednesday. He got so sick that his Mama took him to the hospital emergency room, an' he stayed there at the hospital.

When I got up for school on Thursday morn'n, Mama was in the kitchen on the phone. She was pray'n an' cry'n an' pray'n some more. I got scared. I know someth'n was wrong, but I didn't know what until Mama got off the phone an' she saw me stand'n there. She told me Mo was really sick, his kidneys was fail'n an' he had went into a coma. I started cry'n an' Mama started cry'n again.

I didn't feel much like go'n to school after Mama told me 'bout Mo be'n in a coma an' his kidneys not work'n. So I pretended I was go'n to school, but I rode my bike to the lake to see Jimmy an' tell him 'bout Mo. Funny thing though, Jimmy already knew 'bout Mo be'n sick an' at the hospital, an' in a coma.

I didn't really understand 'bout Mo be'n so sick, so Jimmy explained how Mo's kidneys is suppose to work an' what happened to his body when they didn't work. Jimmy had saw a lot of sick children when he was do'n missionary work an' travel'n to all those faraway places.

We just stared at the water for a long time without

say'n a word. Then I told Jimmy I was gonna find Mo's daddy! Jimmy give me his map. He had circled Eutaw, an' traced a line to Selma, circled also. He wrote the bus number an' schedule on the map, an' he give me ten dollars for a round trip ticket from Eutaw to Selma an' back—with two dollars for me to get someth'n to eat. Jimmy was always there to help me, kinda like a big brother or a dad—except Jimmy was White.

On Friday, I asked Mama could I go to the hospital with her after school to see Mo. She say yes. When Mama an' me got to the hospital, I was really nervous 'cause I never been to a hospital before. But when we got to Mo's room, Mama an' me was both surprised, 'cause Champ was ly'n on the floor next to Mo's bed. Champ saw me. He jumped up an' almost knocked me down. He was so happy to see me!

But the nurse come runn'n when she heard all the noise. She say Champ wasn't suppose to be there but they couldn't get him to move away from Mo's bedside. Champ had rode in the car when Mo's mama drove him to the hospital on Wednesday. He jumped out the window an' followed them into the hospital. Mo's mama talked the hospital nurse into not call'n the animal control people, an' to lett'n Champ stay, as long as he had been good an' quiet. That was, until he saw me.

Mo was still in a coma though, so Mama an' Ms. Rosie Mae prayed an' prayed. Then her an' Mama talked for a long while. When Mama an' me started to leave, Champ got up an' walked out with me. So I asked Mama an' Ms. Rosie Mae if Champ could come home with us that night. They both say yes.

Now I was really determined to find Mo's daddy even more! I studied the map Jimmy give me, all night. I looked at all the places between Eutaw an' Selma until I fell asleep—with Champ ly'n right there beside my bed.

The day before the Atlanta church conference

Mama had finally gave in to Pastor Winewright. He pressed for her to go with him to the big church conference in Atlanta on Saturday (tomorrow) an' Sunday. Mama was a really good secretary an' Pastor say he really needs her there to help him with his presentation.

Mama told me that she arranged for me to stay the night on Saturday with Uncle Wayne an' Auntie Shirley. Mama say that after my chores on Saturday an' after I eat lunch I was to ride my bike over to they house, an' to take a change of clothes for Sunday school the next day. Mama say she was gonna be gone before I woke—head'n for Atlanta with Pastor Winewright—an' she would be back home on Sunday.

I was so excited 'bout tomorrow—go'n to find Mo's daddy—I could hardly sleep! I thought that if I can find Mo's daddy an' come back to the hospital an' tell Mo, he'd wake up from the coma 'cause he would be so excited to see his daddy!

When morn'n come, sho-enough, like Mama say, she was already gone to the big church conference in Atlanta when I woke up. She left a note for me with Uncle Wayne an' Auntie Shirley's phone number on it.

Mama had stopped by Mo's house Thursday night to get dog food for Champ when we was come'n home from see'n Mo at the hospital. I give Champ his food, then poured me a bowl of Cheerios an' milk. When I finished eat'n, I made me a peanut butter an' jelly sandwich an' poured some dog food in a little bag an' I put 'em in my backpack with the map an' money that Jimmy give me for the trip to Dallas County. Then I cleaned up my room an' the kitchen really fast.

It was only eight-thirty a.m. an' Champ an' me was ready to go to town (Eutaw) to catch that first bus at ten o'clock to Selma, in Dallas County, where Mo's daddy live. Champ kept up with me the whole time I was ride'n my bike as fast as I could to town. It was 'bout five miles an' we didn't stop or rest until we got to town.

Jimmy say that if I miss that ten o'clock bus an' have to catch the twelve o'clock bus, I might not have enough time when I get to Selma to find Mo's daddy, 'cause I have to be back home before dark.

Flashback to the lake—Jimmy in the present

The day when Mo and Oli were at the lake with Jimmy and they both asked Jimmy why he didn't go to Vietnam with their daddies and Jimmy got really quiet, Jimmy was remembering the time when he was growing up. He was eleven years old, about Oli's age. Thomas let Jimmy be on his baseball team. Jimmy wasn't very good, but Thomas (an all-around athlete) let Jimmy play anyway.

Flashback—Jimmy at eleven years old

With no one on base and two outs in the bottom of the sixth inning—down by one run—it was Jimmy's time to bat. Jimmy had already struck out two times. Thomas called Jimmy back to the warm-up circle. Jimmy thought he was going to be replaced, but Thomas gave him a pep talk to try and give Jimmy confidence in being able to hit the ball. After two bad swings and misses, Thomas called

48

him back over. "This time," he told Jimmy, "close your eyes and remember what I taught you last summer. Relax, take a deep breath and throw your hands and bat at the ball."

Flashback to the summer before—
Jimmy at ten years old

"Relax, breathe, bring the bat as far back while looking at the ball coming out of the pitcher's hand. Take the bat back a little more, step forward with your left foot and swing the bat across the middle of the plate as fast as you can, while looking at the ball coming to the plate. Now open your eyes. Okay, you're ready," said Thomas. "Now go dig in and hit that ball." Sure enough, Jimmy hit the ball all the way to the fence for a double.

Thomas was the next batter. He came up to the plate and hit a home run to win the game. Thomas had taught Jimmy how to hit a baseball that summer and he had also taught Jimmy how to better understand math, which made it easier for him to do.

Downtown Eutaw
(Bus Station and Ride)

The man at the bus station say my ticket to go to Selma an' come back home was eight dollars an' that I had to keep Champ on the floor in front of me on the bus, an' not on the seat. Champ is a big dog, so I don't know if that's gonna work so good. He say the bus was gonna leave in twenty-five minutes, so me an' Champ walked across the street from the bus stop an' I bought me a soda pop to take on the bus.

I think that bus musta stopped at every town on the map, 'cause that ride was so long, I fell asleep two times. But we finally got there in Selma. Champ was glad to get off the bus, too, 'cause he wanted to climb up on the seat an' look out the window the whole time. But I was afraid the bus driver would get mad an' kick us off the bus, 'cause I had my bike an' Champ, an' we was take'n space for two people.

I'm glad the bus was only half full though, 'cause when we first got on the bus, the driver wasn't gonna let me get on with Champ an' my bike. But I told him that my grandmama was really sick an' I was bring'n her dog back to her 'cause she was better now. I know that was not the truth, but I think God would understand—I was try'n to help Mo by find'n his daddy.

Then the bus driver say okay, but I had to put my bike right next to my seat an' Champ in front of my seat. I didn't know what I was gonna tell him if he be the same bus driver come'n back home to Eutaw, 'cause Champ would still be with me go'n home.

Downtown Selma

Sheriff Gilmore in Eutaw say to Mo an' me, Mo's daddy live in Dallas County. He give Mo a piece of paper with the address, 1315 Lapsley Street in Selma, Alabama. As soon as Champ an' me got off the bus, I opened the map Jimmy give me. I kept turn'n it around until I figured just where we was stand'n on the map. Yep, I got it figured out. "We go that way to Mo's daddy's house," I say to Champ.

I jumped on my bike an' started ride'n through town with Champ runn'n beside me. Selma was kinda like Eutaw, but bigger. There was this great big bridge, Champ an' me was cross'n at the end of the town. It went high, right over a river down below.

When we got on the other side, I pulled out the map again. When I figured where we was at on the map, we was go'n the wrong way. We was suppose to be go'n the other way—north—but instead we was go'n south, toward the city called Montgomery, Alabama on the map. When we turned around to go back, I say real loud, "Oh my goodness!" 'Cause this is the bridge Mama told me 'bout—the bridge on that day when Mama an' daddy an' Mo's mama marched with Dr. Martin Luther King, Jr. They had to turn around, just like Champ an' me have to turn around now! Now I know that we just crossed over the Alabama River, 'cause that's what

Mama an' daddy had did.

I'm excited, but I can't tell Mama that I rode the bus by myself all the way to Selma look'n for Mo's daddy. But here I am! On the same bridge Mama was on—Champ an' me!

Well, I was pretty hungry by now; I think Champ was, too. So we just sat at the bottom of that bridge. I give Champ his food on a napkin from my backpack, an' I ate my sandwich.

Now we was ready to go find Mo's daddy's house. Go'n back over the bridge I see a big sign on the top of the bridge—it say "Edmund Pettus Bridge."

Back in town I see a big clock on a build'n an' it say it's almost one o-clock. Now I know we gonna have to hurry an' find Mo's daddy 'cause the bus that Jimmy say we gotta get on to come back home leave at four-thirty p.m.—an' that will get us home in plenty of time before dark.

It was then I remembered I had forgot to call Uncle Wayne an' Auntie Shirley an' tell them I would be come'n to their house late, 'cause I was gonna stop at the hospital, after all my chores an' homework was done. So I started look'n for a pay telephone so I could call them before they started worry'n 'bout me.

Uncle Wayne was always easy to talk to, 'cause he wouldn't ask a lot of questions. Uncle Wayne answered the phone. I told him the story why I was gonna be late, an' he say, "Just be safe riding your bike over here, babe."

Finally we got to Lapsley Street. Then after go'n three more blocks, I saw the house with 1315 on the mailbox in front. It was on the corner an' two little girls was play'n in the front yard. I asked them if Mr. Wally Wright live here. One little girl run in the house, the other girl say, "Yes, that's my daddy!" I was a little confused at first, but then I realized that Mo have two little sisters! That's so cool!

A man come out the house hold'n the other little girl's hand. "Hello," he say to me. An' I just started tell'n him all 'bout how Mama went to Atlanta an' I was supposed to be at my Uncle Wayne an' Auntie Shirley's house, an' how Mo an' me went down to the sheriff's office that day an' the sheriff say that he had good news, he found Mo's daddy's address in Dallas County an'…

Mo's daddy say, "Hold on now, little angel—slow down—come, let's sit here on the porch and you can tell me all about what brings you to my home." He told the bigger girl, he called Jacqueline, to go in the house an' get a glass of water for me an' a plastic bowl of water for Champ. I didn't even notice until he took the glass of water to hand it to me, that Mr. Wright only had one hand.

Then I remembered what Mama was say'n 'bout when Mo's daddy come home from the Vietnam War.

She say he had changed. He was injured from the war an' how he was mean—drink'n an' always fight'n with Mo's mama. It made me a little nervous think'n 'bout that, but he didn't look mean—or act mean. He was smile'n an' he was be'n real nice.

I don't know where I stopped tell'n Mr. Wright 'bout Mo an' me. So I started tell'n him how Mo an' me been look'n for our daddies for as long as I can remember. So when we got this address from the sheriff in Eutaw, Mo an' me started plann'n to go to Dallas County so Mo could find his daddy. Before I could tell him 'bout Mo be'n sick, he stopped me, an' asked, "Are you Virginia and Thomas's little girl?"

"Yes sir," I say, "but I never met my daddy either." I pulled the picture out my backpack with Mama, daddy, Mo's mama an' daddy, that I always carry with me, an' I showed it to Mr. Wright.

He looked, then he turned an' called out loud into the house for Johnnie Mae—his wife—to come out to the porch. A tall, beautiful, brown-skinned lady come out onto the porch. He asked me my name, then he told her, "This is Olivia, Thomas Jones's little girl. Honey, he was my best friend growing up in Greene County. In fact, I owe him my life."

54

Wally Wright paused for a while, looking at the picture, reflecting back.

Wally Wright's flashback—Vietnam

Wally is in a foxhole with his platoon under heavy gun fire. He sees Thomas crawl out of the foxhole with a bayonet in both hands. Suddenly a grenade explodes in close proximity to him in the foxhole. Soldiers are killed and Wally is seriously injured. There's confusion and panic. His platoon is pinned down under extreme gunfire. A medic attends Wally's injuries.

It suddenly goes silent...Long moments later, Thomas appears. He's standing in the open, looking down into the foxhole where Wally is being treated. Thomas is covered in blood. Thomas had crawled to the Vietcong's position and engaged them in hand-to-hand combat. He had killed all seven or eight Vietcong soldiers, saving his platoon and Wally.

Wally Wright is back to the present moment

"He saved my life when we were in Vietnam. Yes, Olivia, your daddy is an incredibly strong and brave man. He's my hero!" exclaimed Mr. Wright.

I didn't know what to say after he told me that, 'cause

I started daydream'n 'bout meet'n my daddy one day. I want him to be my hero, too.

I snapped out the daydream when Ms. Johnnie Mae asked me if I was hungry, an' to come into the house. She introduced me to the little girls, Jacqueline an' Patricia. Jacqueline was eight years old an' Patricia was six years old. Ms. Johnnie Mae had some fried chicken, macaroni an' cheese, greens an' cornbread. It made me so hungry, I forgot that I had a peanut butter an' jelly sandwich at the bridge. So I say, "Yes ma'am, I would like to eat."

The food was so good. I was happy. It was like this was my family. I kinda forgot why I was there.

Ms. Johnnie Mae told us children to go outside an' play while she cleaned up, an' that she had some dessert for us later. I looked at Mo's daddy an' he smiled an' nodded his head for me to go on outside with Jacqueline an' Patricia.

Outside, we started play'n hopscotch an' then double-dutch jump rope. Suddenly Champ started bark'n an' bark'n until Mo's daddy come out. Then Champ stopped bark'n. Champ's bark'n made me remember why I traveled all morn'n to get to Dallas County to find Mo's daddy an' tell him 'bout Mo be'n so sick an' in a coma at the hospital.

When I finished tell'n Mo's daddy 'bout Mo an' how he got really sick, I told him that's why I wanted to come to Dallas County to find him. So when I tell Mo that I found his daddy, he would be so happy, he would get well an' wake up out of that coma.

Mr. Wright told us to come back in the house. While we was eat'n apple pie dessert, Mo's daddy was tell'n Ms. Johnnie Mae what I told him 'bout Mo an' me.

"Oh no!" I say. "Is that clock on the wall the right time?" It was three-forty an' the bus was leave'n for Eutaw at four-thirty. I told Mo's daddy me an' Champ had to leave. He say calmly, "Don't worry, Olivia," 'cause he was gonna drive me an' Champ back home. He say we would leave around four-thirty an' I would be home long before it got dark.

Now I just wish that Mo could have come to Selma an' be here with his family. I was hope'n he can someday, an' feel the love I feel right here in his daddy's home.

When four-thirty come, Mr. Wright say it was time to go. I say goodbye to Mo's little sisters an' Ms. Johnnie Mae. Then me an' Champ, we get in Mo's daddy's pickup truck an' we drive off, headed for home.

While Mr. Wright was drive'n us home, I asked him 'bout my daddy an' if he knew where my daddy live? He started tell'n me 'bout him an' daddy go'n to the war in Vietnam together, an' how bad it was. He say it was hard for him to think 'bout it, 'cause it was really bad. The things they saw happen over there, an' the things they had did to survive…

Mr. Wright say after he got injured—lose'n his arm

at the elbow—he lost contact with my daddy. He think my daddy got injured on that day, too, while save'n the men that was with their platoon. But he didn't really know 'cause he didn't see him at the hospitals he had been taken to.

He say my daddy had become really close with their sergeant, Ernie Yoholo. He say, if anyone knows how to find your daddy, Sergeant Yoholo would know.

I rode for a while, think'n 'bout my daddy, then think'n 'bout Mo.

I asked Mr. Wright if we could stop by the hospital when we got to Eutaw, so I could see Mo. He say he was plann'n on stopp'n at the hospital to see Mo after he dropped me an' Champ home. But he say he will stop at the hospital first so I can see Mo, too.

Atlanta, Georgia

Virginia was having a terrible time in Atlanta at the church convention. Pastor Winewright's wife had shown up and started a ruckus by accusing Virginia of trying to sleep with the Pastor. Virginia told her that she was married to Thomas. That's when Ms. Winewright told Virginia that Thomas was never coming home, and that Virginia was a fool for wearing her wedding ring all these years.

Virginia retreated to her room. She was upset about what Ms. Winewright had said about her being a fool for wasting her time and lying to herself about still being married to Thomas.

Olivia remembers

I think what really hurt was that Mo's mama had say the same thing 'bout daddy not come'n back home to Mama. It was one night when she was try'n to get Mama to go out to a party with her on New Year's Eve. She told Mama that she was waste'n her time wait'n on Thomas, an' that he was just like Wally—Mo's daddy. He wasn't come'n back home either. Mama got so mad that night, she threw Mo's mama out our house.

Fade back to present day Atlanta

Determined to keep her dignity and not let Ms. Winewright bully or intimidate her, Virginia left her room for the convention delegation meeting to do the work she came to Atlanta to do for Pastor Winewright. Despite the lie and rumors swirling around the convention about Virginia and Pastor Winewright, Virginia did an admirable job keeping the minutes and moving Pastor's agenda forward to a successful conclusion.

Later that evening, Virginia reflected on how hard it had

been raising Olivia all by herself for the past ten or eleven years without Thomas to share in all the ups and downs of raising a little girl. *Was I a fool for believing that one day I would have a complete family, with our daughter, Olivia, and my husband, Thomas?*

All of Virginia's hopes were kept alive years before when Olivia and Mo found the box Thomas had left buried in her backyard next to that big cedar pine tree. Her intuition and faith told her that he was okay. He was somewhere, and God would prevail in bringing him home.

Eutaw, Alabama—County Hospital

When we get to the hospital, I opened the truck door. Champ jumped out the truck an' ran to the hospital door entrance. He waited to go inside with me an' Mo's daddy. Then he took off runn'n to Mo's room.

The nurse told Mo's daddy that Ms. Wright, Mo's mama, had just left the hospital right before we get there. I think Mo's daddy was a little happy that Mo's mama had already left.

The nurse say Mo was improve'n nicely. He was no longer in a coma, but he was rest'n 'cause of the medicine the doctor give him. The whole time we was there, Mo was asleep—just like when he was in a coma.

Dr. Wynn entered the room—then he an' Mo's daddy left out together talk'n 'bout Mo's condition. A little while later when Mo's daddy come back into the room, he had a really serious an' a little bit sad look on his face. He walked to the window an' just stared out for a while.

Then he turned, walked over to Mo's bedside, leaned over an' kissed Mo on the forehead. Then he say it was time to get me home. Me an' Champ say goodbye to Mo, even though Mo was still sleep'n. Then we all left.

While we was drive'n to Uncle Wayne an' Auntie Shirley's house, I wanted to ask Mr. Wright some more 'bout my daddy. But then he just started talk'n an' tell'n me that he tried to tell my daddy 'bout mama be'n pregnant with me, when they was in Vietnam.

But he say daddy had a real strong belief—or superstition—that the less he knew 'bout what was go'n on back home in the States, the better his chance of survive'n the Vietnam War. He saw too many young guys get killed 'cause their minds was on things back home, an' not one-hundred an' ten percent over there in the war.

"The problem though, it makes you a little crazy to be so focused like that over there," he mused out loud. He say he had heard that when daddy come back to the States—after his first tour—he stayed on base until they sent him back for a second tour.

"So when your mama sent letters to Thomas—over there—he would just smell them with his eyes closed.

Then he would walk away without open'n them," he say.

Mr. Wright looked at me with a serious face, then he say, "Olivia, I don't think your daddy knows that he has a beautiful little girl. The war changed us. We saw and did some things that no one should have to see or do. Your daddy started believing that your mama deserved someone better than him. He was very troubled by who he thought he had become." Mr. Wright paused for a moment, then he say, "Your daddy is a good man!" An' he say he was gonna help me find my daddy.

But first he was gonna have to find Sergeant Yoholo for me. He asked me for my address so that he could send the information he finds out 'bout Sergeant Yoholo to me when he get it. 2211 Springfield Road, Eutaw, Greene County, Alabama 35461. I got so happy! Maybe I can really find my daddy, too.

Greene County

When we get to Uncle Wayne an' Auntie Shirley's house, there was a house full of people. Auntie Shirley was fry'n fish that Uncle Wayne had caught an' cleaned at the lake. They was have'n a fish fry'n party. People was play'n cards an' dominoes. The music was loud, play'n the Blues.

Uncle Wayne didn't see me come in the house, but

when Mr. Wright walked in, Uncle Wayne stopped play'n his dominoes, stood up an' shouted, "Wally!" He was so happy to see Mo's daddy. I had forgot that they all growed up together. Uncle Wayne was my daddy's little brother, so he was a little younger than Mr. Wright. I didn't even have to explain where I was all day, they was so happy to see Mr. Wright. They just started talk'n an' laugh'n an' eat'n fish. I fed Champ an' then I had me some fish, too. I musta fallen asleep right after that 'cause I don't know when Mo's daddy left to go back home. But when I woke up it was Sunday morn'n. I think Auntie Shirley musta carried me to bed. I had put Mr. Wright's telephone number in my pocket—he told me I could call him anytime I want.

Auntie Shirley made me some grits, eggs an' fish for breakfast before I rode my bike to Sunday school—me an' Champ. Mama say Auntie Shirley is a atheist, 'cause she don't believe in God—that's why she don't never go to church. I was think'n, maybe Mama was gonna be home for church service today, 'cause she don't like me miss'n Sunday church service. So I was gonna go to church service right after Sunday school. Mama would be happy to see me there.

When the Sunday school was over, I went out where

Champ always be lay'n down wait'n for Mo an' me. But Champ wasn't there, he was gone! I ran all the way around the church an' no Champ anywhere. I got on my bike an' rode as fast as I could back to Uncle Wayne an' Auntie Shirley's house. But when I got there, there was no Champ. Then I rode my bike to my house—nope—he was not there either.

Now I was really scared that Champ ran away—or maybe someth'n bad happen to him—'cause Mo really loves his dog, an' now he's gone! Where could he go? Uh oh, maybe he ran away to go see Mo? Yeah, maybe that's where he went.

I don't know how fast I was ride'n my bike, but I got to the hospital really fast. When I got inside Mo's room, there was Mo's mama an' Champ. An' Mo was sitt'n up in the bed talk'n an' smile'n. I was so happy! Mo was better an' Champ was there an' not lost. Maybe Mo was well now?

I wanted to tell Mo 'bout me find'n his daddy, so bad. But his mama would know that I went all the way to Dallas County on the bus by myself. She would probably be upset. An' I know she would tell Mama an' she would be really mad, 'cause I was supposed to be over Uncle Wayne an' Auntie Shirley's on Saturday. So I had to wait an' tell Mo later the good news 'bout his daddy come'n to the hospital.

Champ stayed at the hospital with Mo an' Ms. Rosie

Mae. It was too late for me to go to church service, so I headed home from the hospital on my bike. Besides, my dress was all dirty from all that ride'n.

Mama was home! I was so happy to see her an' she was happy to see me, too! I wanted to start tell'n Mama all 'bout my adventures to find Mo's daddy in Dallas County, an' how me an' Champ crossed over on the same bridge her an' Daddy was on in Selma. But I had to hold it all in. I thought I was gonna explode if I didn't tell her, but I held it all in me.

So I asked Mama how was her trip to the church conference in Atlanta? Mama didn't have a lot to tell me 'bout her trip to Atlanta or the church conference. But she did say she was very happy to be back home an' that she wasn't go'n to another church conference anytime soon. I don't think Mama had a good time at all.

I told Mama 'bout Mo be'n better, sitt'n up in bed, talk'n, an' how I lost Champ after Sunday school, but then found him at the hospital with Mo an' Ms. Rosie Mae. Mama just laughed an' say, "Honey, is that why you so dirty, chase'n after that dog?" She say, "That dog has a mind of his own, but look how God works Olivia, Champ musta knew Mo was gett'n better!"

On Monday, Mama say we can go see Mo at the hospital when I get home from school. So after school when I get home, me an' Mama went to the hospital. When we went into Mo's room, Ms. Wright an' Champ was already there. Mo was awake an' talk'n, but he had all those tubes go'n from a machine to his body. Mama an' Ms. Wright was busy talk'n while they was sitt'n over by the window. So I whispered to Mo that I found his daddy, an' that his daddy drive me an' Champ back home from Dallas County. I told him that his daddy come to the hospital, but he was asleep 'cause the nurse gave him some medicine that made him sleep.

Mo surprised me 'cause he say in a loud voice, "I know! My daddy was here. He come to see me 'cause my mama told me he was here while I was sleep'n."

Well, Mo said it so loud that Mama an' Ms. Wright stopped talk'n when they heard Mo talk'n 'bout his daddy. Then Ms. Wright started tell'n Mama all 'bout Mo's daddy come'n to the hospital to see 'bout Mo. The nurse had told Mo's mama 'bout Mr. Wright visit'n after she had left. Ms. Wright say that she was glad Mo's daddy come to see 'bout his son, an' that he stayed an' talked to the doctor 'bout Mo's asthma condition an' what it's do'n to his organs. She say he was really concerned 'bout his son.

Her an' Mama walked out the room talk'n, when Mama asked her 'bout Mo's condition. I don't think they wanted me to hear what they was say'n. When they come back, Mama had a serious look on her face, an' she was a little sad, too. We stayed a little while longer, then we left go'n home.

When we was in the car, Mama told me the doctor told Ms. Wright that both Mo's kidneys had stopped work'n an' he was gonna need a new kidney from a donor. An' they don't know when or if they will be able to get Mo a new kidney. Mama started to get emotional—and that made me start to cry—think'n 'bout Mo be'n so sick.

On Tuesday, it was hard go'n to school an' not be'n able to see Mo there all day. So the next day on Wednesday after school I rode my bike to the hospital to see Mo an' finish tell'n him 'bout when me an' Champ rode the bus to Dallas County to find his daddy.

I was so surprised when I went in Mo's room an' there was Mo's mama an' his daddy! Mo's daddy come back to meet with the doctor 'bout Mo's condition. I knew it! Mo was so happy to see his daddy! But the nurse had to give him some medicine to calm him 'cause he was make'n himself sick when he was so excited.

When Mo's mama was talk'n to the nurse, Mo's daddy walked over to me an' handed me a piece of paper all folded up. When I unfolded it, it had Sergeant Ernie Natan Yoholo, an address—5585 Harborside Road—an' a phone number written on it. Mr. Wright whispered to me that he talked to Sergeant Yoholo, an' that my daddy works for him at the shipyard in Mobile, Alabama.

He found my daddy! I couldn't hardly breathe when he told me that 'bout my daddy. I just couldn't believe he found my daddy so fast, 'cause me an' Mo been look'n for so long to find my daddy. I just couldn't believe it! Now my mind was race'n, I couldn't sit still. I wanted to go find my daddy right then!

I saw how happy Mo was to be with his daddy, I just wanted to find my daddy, too! I quietly thanked Mo's daddy, an' then told Mo's mama goodbye. I had to be go'n back home before Mama be worried, 'cause she didn't know that I rode my bike to the hospital, an' I should have already been home from school by now.

On the way home all I could think 'bout was my daddy, an' where was Mobile, Alabama? But I do know who know—Jimmy do! So I know I can't go to school the next day 'cause I gotta go find Jimmy at the lake.

Thursday morn'n I jump on my bike an' head straight to the lake to find Jimmy. I never asked Jimmy why he always be at the lake. But I found out that when

Jimmy's daddy died, he left Jimmy with some land an' a lot of money in his will. So Jimmy didn't have to go to work every day. Instead he come to the lake to read an' meditate—someth'n he learned when he lived in Boston with his auntie. He say meditation helps him to clear his mind an' spirit.

There was Jimmy's car! When I got in the car, I was so excited to tell Jimmy 'bout Mo's daddy find'n where my daddy is, I didn't even see that Jimmy had a map in his hand that say Mobile, Alabama on it. I started tell'n him 'bout my daddy live'n in Mobile, Alabama. Jimmy just smiled at me an' he handed me the map—with Mobile circled in red on the map. I asked him how did he know? How did he know 'bout my daddy live'n in Mobile before I told him so?

Then he told me that he went to the hospital yesterday to see how Mo was do'n an' Wally—Mo's daddy—was there an' that Wally told him 'bout me come'n to Selma to find him for Mo. That's when he told Jimmy that he had some good news for me 'bout my daddy, an' he told Jimmy my daddy lives in Mobile, Alabama. So Jimmy already knew that I was gonna be come'n to the lake to find him for help.

I asked Jimmy, where is Mobile? When Jimmy told me how far Mobile is from Eutaw (one hundred and sixty-six miles) I thought to myself, I can't ride my bike that far! He say it's 'bout three hours by car. After hear'n 'bout that, it made me a little sad. How was I gonna go to Mobile, an' it be that far away?

I was just stare'n at the map where Jimmy circled Mobile. Then Jimmy say he could take me there—to Mobile, Alabama—to find my daddy! I got all excited again an' asked him, "So can we go to Mobile on Saturday?" Jimmy say, well that all depends on how early we can leave Greene County, 'cause he say it will take all day to go to Mobile for a few hours, then drive back to Greene County before dark.

I started think'n, well I always have to get up really early—'bout four-thirty in the morning—when I go fish'n at the lake with Uncle Wayne. So maybe we can leave early like when we be go'n fish'n? "That's it!" I say to Jimmy. I can tell Mama I'm go'n fish'n with Uncle Wayne, 'cause he always be go'n fish'n on the weekend. An' then I could be gone all day, an' Mama wouldn't know I was gone to Mobile. Besides Mama usually go to the church on Saturday to help get it ready for Sunday service. An' sometime Mama stay late when she have to print up the church bulletins. I don't like ly'n to Mama, but if she knew I was try'n to find my daddy, she would be mad an' make me stop. So I asked God to forgive me for ly'n to Mama 'bout go'n fish'n with Uncle Wayne, when I was really go'n to Mobile to find my daddy... Amen!

Jimmy say that's a good plan, but we don't have to

leave as early, like when I go fish'n with Uncle Wayne. He say we can leave at seven a.m. So he tell me to meet him at the lake at six forty-five in the morn'n on Saturday. I took the map of Mobile, Alabama home with me, think'n 'bout my daddy live'n there in Mobile.

On Friday I was excited at school all day, 'cause I asked Mama if I could go fish'n with Uncle Wayne on Saturday, an' she say yes. An' I asked if we could go see Mo at the hospital after I get home from school, an' she say yes, too. As soon as I get home, I asked Mama can we go see Mo!

When we get to the hospital, I guess I shouldn'ta been surprised to see Champ an' Mo's mama already there when me an' Mama went into Mo's room—but I was surprised! Champ an' Ms. Wright was happy to see me an' Mama come'n into the room.

While Mama an' Ms. Wright was talk'n, I quietly told Mo that I was go'n to Mobile, Alabama to find my daddy. An' that his daddy give me Sergeant Ernie Yoholo's address in Mobile, Alabama, 'cause he know where my daddy live! Mo got really happy for me! But he was sad, too, 'cause he really wished he could go with me. So he say to me, take Champ with you to go find your daddy.

So I asked Mama if Champ could come home with me tonight an' go to the lake fish'n with me an' Uncle Wayne. Ms. Wright already say okay, an' so did Mama. I just know God is gonna forgive me for not tell'n Mama the truth. So when me an' Mama left the hospital, Champ come home with us.

Mama was quiet with a worried look when we drove home from see'n Mo at the hospital. I was so excited 'bout go'n to Mobile in the morn'n, I didn't think 'bout why Mama looked worried. But it turned out Ms. Wright told Mama that Mo was gonna have to have surgery on his kidneys in the morn'n. So Mama was silently pray'n an' talk'n to God while she was drive'n us home.

She thought it was better for me not to know Mo was gonna have surgery tomorrow 'cause she didn't want me to worry all night. So Mama thought it was good that I was gonna be at the lake fish'n with Uncle Wayne all day Saturday, instead of be'n at home worried 'bout Mo's surgery.

When we get home I packed my backpack with Champ's food an' some snacks for me. I remember how hungry I was when I went on the bus to Dallas County, so I was make'n sure I had enough food for me an' Champ.

Morn'n come so fast, but I was excited when my alarm clock went off at five forty-five a.m., I jumped straight up out the bed. I think I scared Champ. When I went in the kitchen, I thought I would see Mama, 'cause she always up early, but she was still sleep'n. So I got dressed, fed Champ an' ate a banana an' a bowl of cereal. Then I made me a peanut butter an' jelly sandwich, wrapped it in foil paper an' put it in my backpack with the map, snacks an' dog food. Champ an' me was out the door at six twenty-five a.m. The lake was 'bout four miles away, so we can get there in 'bout twenty or thirty minutes.

There was Jimmy's car. Jimmy put my bike in the car, an' me an' Champ got in. We was ready to go an' Jimmy say it was six fifty-five by the time on his watch.

The drive to Mobile was so long. I never been anywhere that far before. I fell asleep right away. Jimmy drove for a long time, then he had to stop to get some gas. That's when I woke up an' asked Jimmy was we in Mobile? He just laughed an' say no, we were only halfway there.

Jimmy started drive'n again. After a little while he looked over at me an' say he had someth'n he needed to tell me 'bout my daddy. Jimmy started tell'n me that

73

he an' my daddy was friends when they was little—
even though back then they wasn't supposed to 'cause
Jimmy's White. He say it was my daddy taught him to
understand math really good, an' how to make math
easy. An' that's why Jimmy can teach me math—'cause
it was my daddy who showed him how.

Jimmy was tell'n me he used to stutter really bad
when he was my age, an' the White kids used to tease
an' bully him all the time. But my daddy didn't do that.
He say my daddy even picked him to be on his baseball
team even though Jimmy didn't play very well. Then
Jimmy stopped talk'n for a little while.

His voice changed—it was lower—like he was
whisper'n. He say that him an' my daddy was horse-
play'n around while they was walk'n through the
woods one night on their way home. They was a little
older than me an' Mo—'bout thirteen an' fourteen years
old—when they saw a boy be'n lynched by a mob of the
Ku Klux Klan. Jimmy stopped talk'n, an' we rode for a
while not say'n anyth'n.

Then Jimmy say that him an' my daddy never saw
each other again after that day. He say that's when he
left Greene County to go live with his auntie in Boston. It
was right after they saw that boy gett'n lynched. Jimmy
say, see'n that lynch'n has troubled his mind ever since
that day, an' talk'n 'bout it was really hard.

That's why Jimmy be at the lake all the time, to

meditate. Someth'n he learned to do that relaxed his mind an' gave him peace after he went to live in Boston with his aunt. But he say that later, after he left Greene County, an' was live'n in Boston, he felt like he had ran away to Boston, leave'n my daddy all alone back home to deal with the memory of that boy be'n lynched, there in the town where it happened. Jimmy say he felt like a coward for do'n that to my daddy. But he say he just couldn't stay in Greene County after that lynch'n happened.

We drove the rest of the way in silence. I was stare'n out the window watch'n the trees an' farms pass'n—the sign say Mobile twenty-five miles. I don't know much 'bout lynch'n, but I was remember'n that time Mama an' me was at Uncle Wayne an' Auntie Shirley's house an' someth'n bad happened in the news. 'Cause Uncle Wayne was say'n how bad things useta be for Black people in Alabama an' the South, with a lot of lynch'ns. He say Dr. King was march'n to stop the lynch'n an' unjust treatment of Black people an' to get their freedom in America. He say lynch'n and beat'ns was a way to put fear into Black people, an' stop them from fight'n for their freedoms.

Jimmy broke the silence when he asked me if I think my daddy would forgive him for leave'n like he did, leave'n Greene County without tell'n my daddy? I didn't know what to say, 'cause Jimmy know I never met my daddy, so I don't know. But I thought 'bout it awhile. I remembered what Mama say 'bout how you have to forgive the people who hurt you. She say, "Sometimes they don't even know they hurt you, an' when you don't forgive, it hurts your own soul." She say we want our soul to be pure for God, so we have to forgive!

So I say, "Yes," to Jimmy, "my daddy would forgive you 'cause my daddy would want to have a pure soul for God!" Jimmy just looked over at me, but he didn't say anyth'n else until we get to Mobile.

Once we get to Mobile, Alabama, Jimmy say when we find the address for Sergeant Yoholo that he would wait in the car while I talked to Sergeant Yoholo 'bout my daddy.

I started think'n how Jimmy never told me that he knew my daddy, an' that it was my daddy that taught Jimmy how to do math easy, just like Jimmy been teach'n me. I wanted to ask Jimmy more 'bout my daddy, but he had that same look on his face, like that time me an' Mo asked Jimmy why he didn't go to Vietnam like our daddies did.

So I just stared out the window think'n 'bout my daddy. I was think'n 'bout when Me an' Mo was four and five years old an' we found that box in the backyard when we was digg'n to plant flower seeds, an' when Mama give me the necklace chain from inside the box with my daddy's name—Thomas Jefferson Jones—on the tag. I reached my hand up to my neck to feel the chain.

Mobile, Alabama

Wow! I never seen a big city before. Mobile, Alabama was big—I mean really big! Jimmy asked me if I was hungry when we got to Mobile, but I was too excited to eat so I say no. I asked can we go find my daddy now? He say calm down, first we have to go find Sergeant Yoholo's house an' talk to him, 'cause he's the person who knows how to find my daddy.

Selma, Alabama
(two days earlier)

The test results, to see if Mr. Wright was a match to give Mo a kidney, had come back on Thursday. Wally was a perfect match. The doctor called Wally with the results and told him that they wanted to schedule the surgery as soon as possible. They set it for early Saturday morning, the same morning Oli and Jimmy left for Mobile.

When the doctor first told Mr. Wright that his son was very sick and in desperate need of a kidney, Mr. Wright asked if he could be considered as a candidate to give Mo a kidney. The doctor told him yes, but he should first talk it over with his wife because it was a big family decision. He could only give a kidney once, so if his wife or daughters ever needed, he would not be able to give a kidney to any of them.

When Mr. Wright returned home from taking Oli back to Greene County the previous Saturday, he told Johnnie Mae about Mo's condition and what the doctor said about him being a possible donor. Johnnie Mae immediately agreed that Wally should get tested to see if he could be a match to give his son a kidney.

On Wednesday, Dr. Wynn scheduled Wally to come back to Greene County Hospital to be tested. It was the same day Mr. Wright gave Oli the name and address of Sergeant Yoholo in Mobile, Alabama, helping Oli to find her daddy. It was the reason Mr. Wright was at the hospital when Oli stopped by to see Mo after school, and also the day Jimmy saw Mr. Wright there.

Back in Mobile, Alabama

Jimmy pulled up to the house with the address the same as what Mo's daddy wrote on the paper for Sergeant Yoholo's house. It was a big house with red an' white brick, a black roof, an' a white fence all the way around the land an' house. There was a big, long porch, all the way across the front of the house. It was the prettiest house I ever seen. I told Jimmy I can't go up to that big house by myself! Jimmy just smiled an' say, "Come on, I'm go'n up there with you."

A young man—maybe eighteen or nineteen years old—answered the door. I asked him did Sergeant Yoholo live here? He say, "Yes, that's my father." Jimmy tell him that we needed to speak with Sergeant Yoholo 'bout my daddy, Thomas Jones. The young man tell us to wait there on the porch, he would get his father for us.

He returned a few minutes later with a medium height, stocky built, reddish brown man with little crinkles around his eyes and hair pulled back in a ponytail. He was Native American. "I'm Mr. Yoholo, how may I help you?" he asked. I was so happy I was there 'cause I was excited think'n 'bout, he know where my daddy live! I couldn't talk.

Jimmy told him that I was Olivia Jones, an' that I was try'n to find my daddy, Thomas Jones. "And Wally Wright gave Olivia your address and said you would be able to help us find him," Jimmy say.

Sergeant Yoholo smiled an' told us to come on into his house. He say he was expect'n us, but not this quickly. The inside of the house was more beautiful than I could imagine. The ceil'n was so high above my head with light pour'n in from the tall windows extend'n the outside into the inside. A fireplace open'n as tall as me, made from huge grey stone against the wall of the room Sergeant Yoholo gestured for us to enter. The walls had paint'ns of Native Americans, horses, buffalo skin rugs, an' a portrait of a chief, an' underneath it had the name *Opothle Yoholo—Tuckabatchee Leader.*

He say he talked with Wally on Thursday. He say also that he had lost contact with Wally after Wally got released from the VA hospital an' was discharged from the Army, almost ten years ago. He say how happy he was to hear from Wally, an' to know he was do'n well. But he was very surprised to hear Thomas had a daughter, 'cause Thomas never mentioned it to him.

Wally told Sergeant Yoholo all 'bout me, an' how me an' Mo got his address from the sheriff in Eutaw, an' that I come to Selma to find him to tell him 'bout his son Mo. An' that I asked Wally to help me find my daddy, Thomas. So that's why Sergeant Yoholo say he was expect'n us, but not this soon! He smiled an' kinda laughed to himself.

Then he told us that he an' daddy become good friends while they served in the Vietnam War an' they stayed in touch afterwards. My daddy looked him up in Mobile when daddy got out the Army. He say my daddy first lived here in Sergeant Yoholo's home, when daddy first come to Mobile, Alabama. He paused— look'n at me—he smiled a big smile an' say, "Thomas has a beautiful little girl, and you have his smile! Olivia you are a miracle sent from the heavens, and Thomas doesn't even know of this blessing yet."

He say my daddy works for him on the shipyard at the docks down on the harbor. "Thomas is one of my haulers, with three trucks operating for us." He say that he didn't tell Thomas 'bout him talk'n to Wally. It was a little hard for him to believe it himself, what he was hear'n on the phone 'bout me, in his conversation with Wally—Thomas have'n a little girl!!?? So he thought it was best not to say anyth'n until he actually met me. Now I was fix'n to bust—my daddy work for Sergeant Yoholo!

So I ask, "You know how to find my daddy right now?" He say yes an' I say, "Can we go an' find my daddy now?" I was so excited! Sergeant Yoholo say yes we can, but first he was have'n lunch prepared for us to eat before we go. After that he would call Thomas. Then he would take me to meet my daddy. He say when he talks to Thomas, he will just tell him he has a special person for him to meet...that was me!

I could hardly breathe, think'n 'bout meet'n my daddy. I fed Champ on the porch before I sat down to eat. Then I was eat'n the lunch without think'n 'bout what it was I was eat'n. My mind was race'n. I was think'n 'bout the picture I showed Sergeant Yoholo— with mama, daddy, an' Mo's mama an' daddy. I was wonder'n how my daddy looked now? 'Cause that picture was old, before I was born.

When we finished eat'n lunch, Sergeant Yoholo went

into another room for a little while. When he come back he say he just talked to my daddy an' that he would be wait'n for us.

I don't know how to describe how I was feel'n, but it feel like I was walk'n on a cloud, 'cause my mind was race'n so fast, I don't remember walk'n to Jimmy's car, but when I opened the door an' Champ jumped in he bumped into me. Then I knew, this was not a dream. I'm go'n to see my daddy!

Sergeant Yoholo got in the front seat with me an' Jimmy. Champ was in the back seat where Jimmy first put my bike. He moved my bike out an' put it in the trunk think'n that Sergeant's son was ride'n with us. But Sergeant Yoholo had his son follow us in another car. When Jimmy was drive'n to my daddy's house, what was happen'n in my mind was now happen'n in my belly, just jump'n all around inside. I was gett'n so nervous 'bout meet'n my daddy for the first time!

Jimmy drive for maybe twenty minutes. Then he pulled off the main road onto a dirt road, an' he drive a few minutes more when Sergeant Yoholo tell Jimmy to pull over an' stop. His son pulled his car up behind Jimmy's car an' stopped, too.

Back in Greene County

Mo and Mo's daddy went into surgery at nine o'clock

on Saturday morning. Dr. Wynn told Ms. Rosie Mae and Ms. Johnnie Mae that the doctors were expecting to be in surgery six to seven hours, depending on how everything went. After waiting for just a little while, both Ms. Rosie Mae and Ms. Johnnie Mae decided to go back home and stay busy for awhile, to keep from worrying about the surgery. Ms. Johnnie Mae drove back home to Selma, planning to return to the hospital at around three or four p.m. Ms. Rosie Mae decided to go to the church to see Virginia and Pastor Winewright, and ask for them to pray together for both the surgeries to go well. She also planned to go back to the hospital around three or four p.m.

Back in Mobile, Alabama

Before Sergeant Yoholo get out the car, Jimmy told him we had to leave Mobile for home around two-thirty p.m. but not later than three o'clock, for me to be back home before dark. He assured Jimmy that wouldn't be a problem. Then Sergeant Yoholo asked me to get out the car with him. He told Jimmy to wait there with Champ, then he walked back to his son's car an' told him to also wait there in his car.

We walked up the dirt road for 'bout a half a block. It was around twelve-thirty on a beautiful fall afternoon, temperature seventy to seventy-five degrees. The road had big trees line'n both sides with houses far apart

83

from each other tucked behind the trees. We stopped at a house that had a big sixteen-wheeler tractor trailer truck parked on the property. Sergeant Yoholo say this is where my daddy live.

Now my heart was pound'n so hard an' fast, it feel like it's gonna explode. As we got closer to the house, the front door swing open an' a tall caramel-skinned man with a short afro hair style stood there in the doorway, with a big bright smile on his face.

My mind started think'n this gotta be a dream, 'cause there's an angel stand'n there look'n at me—his eyes as bright as the sun!

Then he spoke, "Hey Sarge, who's the beautiful little angel with you?" Sergeant Yoholo reached out his hand, shook Daddy's hand an' hugged him with the other arm. He say this is the special person I want you to meet. Her name is Olivia. Daddy say, "Hi Olivia, come on inside the house." I know my mouth was open, but no words would come out.

I walked in the house with Sergeant Yoholo. Daddy was right behind me. As soon as we sat down at the table in the middle room, Sergeant Yoholo looked at Daddy an' say, "Thomas, this beautiful little angel is your daughter, Olivia Jones!" It got really quiet in there.

Sergeant Yoholo continued, "I talked to your Army buddy, Wally Wright. He told me that Olivia's mom, Virginia, had written to you several times when you were in Vietnam. He says she was trying to tell you that she was pregnant, and that you were going to be a father. Wally said he tried to tell you, but you refused to know or want to hear about anything going on back home in the States. Thomas, you know how crazy focused you were over there!"

While Sergeant Yoholo was talk'n, I pulled the picture out my backpack an' handed it to daddy across the table. He was look'n a little dazed, like he was there, but he wasn't really.

As daddy stared down at the picture, I could see a tear in his eyes. He looked up at me an' he say, "Baby, I'm so sorry. I'm so sorry, I didn't know! Oh baby, I didn't know about you…My heart has been so broken, because I still love your mama!" When Daddy say that, I just started cry'n, 'cause I was so happy, my daddy still love my mama!

Now I pulled the necklace chain with the tag from around my neck an' handed it to Daddy. Daddy was hold'n the necklace in his hand. Then Daddy started cry'n, an' then we both was cry'n.

When we stopped cry'n, I told Daddy that Mama give me the necklace chain on my birthday. It was that day me an' Mo found that green box buried in the backyard over by that big-o pine tree. Mama give it to me an' say when I wear the necklace chain, with this tag that has Daddy's name on it, "It means your daddy is right here with you, baby, right next to your heart."

I told Daddy that's what Mama say, an' that I don't need to wear the necklace any more 'cause I'm right here now, with you! Daddy smiled an' say, "Yes baby, I'm right here with you, too, right next to your heart, and that's where I'll always be!"

Daddy stood up an' walked over to me with his arms stretched wide open. I stood an' he hugged me an' held me in his arms. I don't know what heaven feel like, but when my daddy hugged me in his arms, it was like I was there—in the warmth an' love—in heaven!

I told my daddy that Mama didn't know I was come'n to Mobile to find him, an' that I told Mama I was go'n fish'n with Uncle Wayne today. But instead of go'n fish'n, Jimmy drive me to Mobile to find him. Then Sergeant Yoholo say to Daddy that I have to leave go'n back home, not later than two-thirty p.m. so I could be back home before Mama gets worried 'bout me. It was already one-forty p.m. I asked Daddy could he come home now? I was so surprised when Daddy say, "Yes, baby, Daddy can come home now."

Daddy excused himself from the room. He say he had to make a couple phone calls an' grab a few things, an' he would ride back home with me.

When daddy come back in the room he had a big green bag over his shoulder. He say, "Lets go, babe. Daddy's hand was so big, both my hands could fit into his one hand. We walked back to Jimmy's car. When we get close to the car Jimmy opened the door an' get out. Champ jumped out an' ran to me an' Daddy. My daddy was so surprised to see Champ, 'cause I forgot to tell him 'bout Mo's dog, Champ. Daddy really liked him. He bent over an' started pett'n him on the head. Funny thing, Champ liked Daddy, too!

Daddy took his attention away from Champ as he stood back up, look'n right at Jimmy. After what seemed like a long time, he say, "Is that Jimmy?" But before I finished say'n yes, Daddy say, real loud, "Jimmy Lee!" Daddy walked up to Jimmy, an' they both stood there for a moment. Then Daddy reached his hand out to Jimmy.

They shook hands. Then Daddy put his other arm around Jimmy an' embraced him with a hug. But they didn't say a word. Then I say to Jimmy, "My daddy gonna ride back home to Greene County with us!" Jimmy say, "That's great! Let me take your bag!" An' he put it in the trunk of his car with my bike.

I give Sergeant Yoholo a big hug an' thanked him for take'n me to find my daddy! When we get in the car, me, Daddy an' Jimmy get in the front seat together with Champ in the back seat. Then we drove off.

By the time we get to the highway, I was so tired from all the excitement—an' this long day—I fell fast asleep, lean'n on my daddy's chest with his big arm around me.

Back in Greene County

Mo and Mr. Wright came out of surgery at three-forty p.m., and were both in recovery. The doctor came out to the waiting room and told Ms. Rosie Mae, Ms. Johnnie Mae and Virginia that the surgery went very well. He said that now it was going to be all about their recovery and how well Mo's body would accept the donor kidney.

When Virginia and Ms. Rosie Mae returned to the hospital, Ms. Johnnie Mae, along with Mo's little sisters, Jacqueline and Patricia, were already there in the waiting room. Pastor Winewright had also come to the hospital to give his support and to have prayer with the families. He stayed awhile, talking with the families about the power of God to heal, and encouraging them with biblical scripture. Everyone was in good spirits when he left, especially after the report by Dr. Wynn that the surgery went very well.

There appeared to be great harmony between the two families as well, each giving support to the other. With both families having a loved one go through this major surgery, it seemed to create a spirit of oneness. Virginia was praying with Ms. Johnnie Mae and Ms. Rosie Mae was spending time talking and comforting both Jacqueline and Patricia, making sure they didn't worry, saying their daddy was going to be just fine, just like Mo was going to be.

On the Highway Back to Greene County

On the drive back to Greene County, while Olivia slept, Jimmy asked Thomas to forgive him for abandoning him and leaving town to go live in Boston with his mom's sister. He told Thomas that he left town immediately after that day they both witnessed that lynching.

Thomas didn't realize that Jimmy left for Boston on his own. He thought Jimmy's father had sent him away. He also thought Jimmy told his dad what they both saw that night.

Jimmy told Thomas he had realized that night, that his father had taken him to a gathering like that before, when Jimmy was a little boy, maybe five or six years old. Jimmy said it traumatized him, and he had been afraid of his father ever since but didn't know why until that night Tony was lynched. Jimmy said that was about the time he could remember he began stuttering, soon after his father had taken him to that gathering.

So when Thomas and Jimmy saw that lynching, it brought back the memory of the trauma Jimmy suffered when he was that little boy. Jimmy said he didn't really remember exactly or even understand what he saw or what was going on but being at that gathering frightened him deeply!

Wow! Thomas could hardly believe what Jimmy was telling him. He could only imagine how difficult and scary it must have been for Jimmy to live in a home where the father was so hateful—and pretending to be God's messenger. Thomas finally said to Jimmy, "Man, I don't need to forgive you; you had to save yourself from that crazy world that you were born into! I'm glad you escaped all that hate. I only wish I could have, too! I thought the Army would be my escape…It wasn't! Vietnam was a long, deadly nightmare… what I saw over there…"

After a few moments, Thomas told Jimmy, "I have a confession to make to you. I need to ask for your forgiveness. I don't know exactly how or why, but I was there the night your father died." Then Thomas told Jimmy all of what had happened that night, how he confronted his father about lynching that boy, Tony. He said Jimmy's father got crazy mad when he told him there was another witness there that night. He had said to Jimmy's father, "Your son, Jimmy, was there, and he saw everything you did to that boy—you lynched him—and the sheriff was there, and he was part of what you did to that boy!"

Thomas continued, "Your father attacked me when I turned and was leaving his house. He struck me across the head with the fireplace iron. When I defended myself…"

Jimmy stopped Thomas in mid-sentence. He had a quizzical look on his face. Then he said, "You're the soldier they were looking for to question about my father's death."

Thomas answered, "Yes, but I knew if I stayed to tell what happened that racist Klan sheriff would have arrested me, and hell, they would have probably lynched me that night, in my Army uniform! Like their Klan friends did to so many other Black soldiers..."

Jimmy said, "My father hurt so many families. I'm just so sorry this happened to your family!" They rode in silence for a long while, both in reflective thought.

When I woke up, we was on the highway headed home. Jimmy was say'n to Daddy that Greene County has changed a lot since Daddy been gone, an' there's a new kinda sheriff in town. Sheriff C. T. Gilmore, a Black man who is fair an' just in how he upholds the law. "Heck, he don't even wear a gun. He's known as the 'sheriff without...'" When Jimmy see I was awake, he stopped talk'n to Daddy an' he say to me, "You had a good nap, we are about an hour away from Greene County."

Daddy say to me, "Baby, I called your Uncle Wayne before we left my house. I haven't talked to my brother in a very long time. I told him that you were in Mobile and that you were okay. I told my brother that I was coming back home to Greene County, and that I would probably need to stay with him and your Aunt Shirley for a while."

He then say that him an' Mama gonna need some time to figure things out, on how we gonna go forward as a family from here on.

Thomas paused, thinking, *It's just so hard to believe that Virginia didn't move on with her life and remarry.*

I didn't really understand 'cause I wanted my daddy to come home with me an' Mama, but Uncle Wayne don't live far, so I just say okay Daddy.

I started think'n 'bout the lie I told Mama when I told her I was go'n fish'n with Uncle Wayne. Now she gonna know the truth when Jimmy an' my daddy take me to my house. Well, Uncle Wayne probably already called Mama after he talked to my daddy. So I know I'm in trouble. Maybe Mama gonna be mad an' happy at the same time, when she see Daddy walk in the door with me.

Then I remembered 'bout Mo be'n in the hospital, an' I wanted him to see my daddy! So I asked Daddy if we can stop at the hospital to see Mo before we go home? Daddy say yes, he would love to meet Mo—if it's okay with Jimmy—Jimmy say yes, of course, we can stop by the hospital an' visit Mo.

Back in Greene County

When we arrived at Greene County Hospital, the time on Jimmy's watch say five forty-five p.m. As soon as I let Champ out, he ran to the hospital door an' waited for it to open, then he ran in look'n for Mo's room. Jimmy come in with us. Him an' Daddy asked the nurse what room Mo was in. The nurse say Mo was in surgery this morn'n, so Mo an' Mr. Wright was upstairs in the recovery room.

Jimmy an' Daddy was a little confused, 'cause the nurse say Mo an' Mr. Wright was in the recovery room? Then the nurse say that Mo had kidney transplant surgery this morn'n, an' Mr. Wright was his donor. She then say that Champ couldn't go in the recovery room with us.

So Jimmy an' me took Champ out an' put him in Jimmy's car to wait while we went back in the hospital to see Mo. I'm think'n—Mo had surgery, an' now he got a new kidney? When we went upstairs to the recovery room, I could not believe what my eyes was see'n, 'cause Mama, Ms. Rosie Mae an' Jacqueline was all in the room. Mo was in the bed with tubes connected to his body an' some machines. But before I could say someth'n to Mama, Daddy walked over to her an' say Mama's name, "Virginia…Virginia, I am so sorry. I didn't know. I'm so sorry. Can you ever find it in your heart to forgive me? I have so much to tell you. I didn't know you were pregnant, I didn't know you were raising our child." The room got really quiet, except for the beep'n come'n from the machines hooked up to Mo.

Mama was so surprised to see Daddy but she didn't say anything. She just stared at Daddy with a tear in her eyes. Then Mama say, "Thomas Jefferson Jones, where have you been? I thought you were dead. I pray for you every night. I prayed for God to keep you safe and keep you well through the Vietnam War. I didn't know what to do or think, when you didn't come home and you hadn't answered my letters. I just prayed to God for the strength to make it through each day. And yes, He has, Thomas! God brought me and Olivia through these past eleven years..."

Mama paused, then she say, "I stopped praying for you, Thomas. But then Olivia and Mo found the metal Army box that you, or God, buried in my backyard. That box was my sign from God that I had been praying to Him for! I asked God to let me know that you were alive, and to bring you back home to me and Olivia. So you see, Thomas, God wouldn't let me stop praying for you to be safe, and praying for Him to bring you back home safely to me and Olivia."

Daddy—with tears in his eyes—stretched out his arms to Mama. But Mama just stood there, she didn't move toward Daddy. Then Ms. Rosie Mae say to Mama,"Virginia, girl, this is what you have been praying for—to have your family together—it's why you still have that wedding ring on your finger, right now!"

Mama started cry'n. An' with tears in his eyes, Daddy stepped closer an' wrapped his arms around Mama. Then I was cry'n, Mo's mama was cry'n, even Jimmy had a tear in his eyes, everybody was cry'n, except Jacqueline, she was just smile'n, but she didn't really understand what was happen'n. Mo was awake but still recover'n. He was medicated for the pain from the surgery.

Me an' Jimmy was stand'n next to Mo when Ms. Johnnie Mae an' Patricia come in the room. Now I understand what the nurse downstairs was say'n when she say Mo an' Mr. Wright was in recovery. It was Mo's daddy who give Mo one of his kidneys so that Mo could be well again.

Ms. Johnnie Mae said that Wally was ask'n how was Mo do'n? She come to Mo's room to check in on him. She say Wally was recover'n very well. Then Mo's mama introduced everybody to each other.

Look'n at everyone in the room, I'm think'n 'bout when I was in Selma at Mo's daddy's house eat'n at the table, an' I was wish'n I had a family like Mo's little sisters did. Well, this night, it feel like I do have that family!

By the time we left the hospital, Mama an' Daddy

had talked for a while. Daddy told Mama that he would be stay'n at Uncle Wayne an' Auntie Shirley's house while him an' Mama figure things out.

Then Daddy say to Jimmy, he want to meet with him on Monday, an' finish the conversation they was have'n in the car earlier today 'bout Sheriff Gilmore. Jimmy say okay. Then we all left Mo's room, except Mo's mama, she stayed. Ms. Johnnie Mae, Jacqueline an' Patricia went back to Mr. Wright's recovery room. We all stopped in to see him before we left the hospital. Mama was so happy to see Mr. Wright. She was so proud of what he did, give'n a kidney to his son. I went over an' squeezed Mr. Wright's hand, an' quietly thanked him for everyth'n he did.

Jimmy got my bike out his car an' put it in Mama's trunk. I put Champ in the back seat of Mama's car. Daddy gave me a big hug, then Jimmy an' Daddy drove off. He was take'n Daddy to Uncle Wayne an' Auntie Shirley's house.

As soon as Mama drove away, she looked over at me, an' she say, "Olivia Lynnette Jones, you have been a busy little girl. Do you realize how dangerous it is for an eleven-year-old little girl to be traveling by herself all across the State of Alabama, and to places like Selma and Mobile?" Then she say, "Baby, you been lying to your mama. I know how much you've wished for your daddy to be home and in your life—only God knows baby, how much I do, too. But baby, you are still just a child..."

Mama reached her hand over an' rubbed my head. Then she say, "Thank you, baby—thank you for bringing your daddy home!" Mama smiled an' say, "We never know how God is gonna work things out, or who He will use to answer our prayers!"

When Monday morn'n come, I was all bubbly inside think'n 'bout see'n my daddy after school 'cause I'm gonna ride my bike to Uncle Wayne's house as soon as I get out of school.

Jimmy picked up Thomas around ten o'clock Monday morning. They drove to Jimmy's spot at the lake and parked.

Thomas asked Jimmy about the new sheriff in Greene County that Jimmy spoke about when they were riding back from Mobile on Saturday. Jimmy told Thomas that Sheriff C. T. Gilmore grew up in Greene County but left. When he returned back home, he had two run-ins with the law—one with a state trooper and the other with a county sheriff.

The sheriff told this story when he ran for the position—twice, first in1966 and again in 1970 when he won the election—and he became the first Black sheriff in Greene County history. Jimmy told Sheriff Gilmore's story to Thomas:

As Gilmore drove his car to the gas station, just after a rain storm, he unknowingly ran into a puddle of water and it splashed a White state trooper. The trooper caught up with Gilmore at the gas station and retaliated by pushing Gilmore against a gas pump and forcing him to wash his car. The other incident happened a little later when Gilmore attempted to file a complaint about a police officer assaulting a Black woman. The county sheriff savagely beat Gilmore in the district attorney's office.

Those two incidents led Gilmore, at the age of twenty-four, to run for sheriff in 1966, which he lost. He ran again in 1970 and won. During his campaign he stated that he had been inspired by the teachings of Dr. Martin Luther King, Jr. Gilmore is known as "The Sheriff Without a Gun."

After a lot of conversation between Jimmy and Thomas—and some catching up on what each other had been doing with their lives—Thomas told Jimmy he wanted to make right the things he caused Virginia and Olivia to go through. He also wanted to stop the feeling he had been carrying, like he had to keep looking back over his shoulders. But first, he had to stop running from his past—the incident with Jimmy's father. They both agreed that Thomas should turn himself in to Sheriff Gilmore.

Jimmy told Thomas about the "will" his father left, leaving him a lot of money and land. He told Thomas that he would post bail, and that he would get Thomas the "best lawyer" out of Montgomery to represent him and argue his case of self-defense.

Thomas asked Jimmy to drive him over to the church where Virginia worked. He wanted to tell her all about what happened the night he came home from the Army—and that he was going to turn himself in to the new sheriff. Thomas now wanted to start his life over with Virginia and Olivia, but first, he had to atone for what he had done.

First Baptist Church

When Thomas and Jimmy arrived at the church, Virginia was in a meeting with Pastor Winewright. She had just confided in the Pastor about Thomas coming back home. So they both were a little surprised when Jimmy and Thomas walked into Pastor's office.

After introductions and a bit of small talk, Thomas said to Virginia, "I know I have a lot to explain about where I've been, and why I didn't come back home to you. And now I know that I should have—at the least—written to you or called you. Virginia, I'm so sorry. But I believed I had to lose myself in Vietnam in order to survive over there, and in doing so, I became a different person, someone I didn't like and I thought I wasn't worthy of having your love." He continued, "The things they made us do to survive were ungodly—nothing you learn in church—I hated who I became! But it was how I was able to make it through the Vietnam War."

Pastor Winewright just stood there, shaking his head in disbelief of the tragedy of war on the men that fought them.

Thomas continued, "Before I got back to the States, I was angry and confused. It was my Sergeant, Ernie Natan Yoholo, who saved my life—not physically, but spiritually and mentally. Sarge is Native American. He introduced me to his spiritual way of life. He taught me how to meditate, and to tap into my inner self and still my mind and the world around me...and how to find moments of peace while even there in the jungles of Vietnam. The things I saw and had to do to survive were constantly troubling my mind and spirit."

"I struggled over what to do when I came back to the States—but I stayed in contact with Sarge; he was my north star, my mental refuge. He knew what I had gone through and what I was battling. Sarge helped me to forgive myself and to make the decision to come back home to you. Baby, I did come home...it's what I've been wanting to tell you."

There was a long pause. Thomas went on, "I came back

to Greene County in the fall of 1970. The bus brought me to downtown Eutaw around seven p.m. As I walked through town headed home to you, I found myself in front of American Southern Baptist Congregation, Pastor Lee's church, when suddenly, in my mind I flashed back to a memory I had suppressed and tried to forget...

"Virginia, you remember that boy, Tony, that was lynched outback in the woods by the old cotton gin, back when we were teenagers? I saw them lynch Tony—me and Jimmy Lee were both there!"

"Oh, my Lord!" gasped Pastor Winewright. Virginia held her hand over her mouth in shock!

"Me and Jimmy both saw a bunch of Klan in white robes all around that boy. He was standing on a big barrel, trembling, with a rope around his neck.

"One of the Klan told another to let him hang! The other Klan then kicked the barrel from under Tony's feet. They hung that boy! They hung that boy right there while we hid in the bushes, scared that they might see us.

"When those two Klan leaders took off their hoods—it was Pastor Lee and the sheriff who did that lynching. They hung that boy! I didn't know what to do or who to tell, so I didn't say anything to anybody. I was afraid of what would happen to me and to anyone I told what they did. I cried almost every day for months for that boy, Tony!

"The night I got into town and found myself in front of the church, I got really angry thinking about what Pastor

Lee did to that boy. I went into the Pastor's side door and confronted him. I told him I knew what he had done to that boy. I told him that I saw him lynch that boy and I was gonna tell what I knew.

"Then I told him that I had a witness that also saw him do it, and that his son, Jimmy, was there with me! He went crazy and struck me with a fireplace iron across my head. When he tried to strike me again, I just remember that I grabbed him by his throat. When he finally stopped struggling to strike me, I let him go. But he fell limp to the floor. He wasn't moving, so I thought he might be dead!"

Thomas stopped to catch his breath, then continued, "I didn't know what to do! But I knew if I stayed to tell what happened, that racist sheriff wouldn't believe me. Besides, he was a Klansman. So, I just ran. I ran all the way to your house Virginia...

"Virginia, I saw you that night, through your back window. But I knew I had to keep running. As a solider, I knew I didn't want to bring any trouble home to your life. It was then, while watching you, that I realized I had been wrong for shutting you out of my personal struggles with life, and oh, how much I really missed you! But Virginia, I didn't know you had a baby—our baby—I just didn't know!"

Then Jimmy interrupted Thomas and said to Virginia, "I'm so sorry this happened to your family. I didn't know who my father really was until that night when I saw him at that lynching. I was traumatized seeing my father murder that boy. I knew I had to leave—how could I face him after that night? I took money from my mom and caught a bus to Boston to stay with my mom's sister. I couldn't be around my father any longer. That night I realized why I had always been afraid of him. After that, I spent years traveling to third world countries doing missionary work. I think I was trying to undo the wrongs of my father by helping others."

Pastor Winewright had everyone form a prayer circle. Then he gave a prayer, and asked God to forgive them for their sins—bring peace in the hearts and minds of these young people, Lord—and to guide Thomas in his decisions going forward...Amen!

Thomas told Virginia and Pastor Winewright he was going to turn himself in to Sheriff Gilmore. He was ready to make amends for what he did. Virginia told Thomas she would stand by him through whatever happened. She walked up and gave Thomas a big hug and said, "I still love you, too, Thomas, I never stopped!"

Thomas told them what Jimmy said about paying for the best defense lawyer he could find in the state of Alabama. Pastor Winewright said that he could help with finding a good lawyer. He grew up in Montgomery and knew some fine attorneys there—attorneys that represented Dr. King and the civil rights movement.

Pastor Winewright had marched as a teenager with Dr. Martin Luther King, Jr., there in Montgomery. His family were members of Dexter Avenue Baptist Church when Dr. King was the Pastor there. In fact, it was Dr. King's inspiration which led Pastor Winewright to go into the ministry. Dr. King had spoken of the unjust power of law enforcement in too many counties, still here in Alabama.

Then Pastor Winewright quoted Dr. King, saying, "Power at its best, is love implementing the demands of justice, and justice at its best is power correcting everything that stands against love."

They all agreed that it would be best if Thomas waited until Thursday morning before going down to the sheriff's office. That would give Jimmy and Pastor time to get an attorney to represent him, before they went down to the sheriff's and the district attorney's offices to surrender Thomas.

On Monday, when I get home from school, it seemed like everybody was at my house—Mama, Daddy, Jimmy, Uncle Wayne an' Auntie Shirley. It was kinda like a family reunion 'cause Mama an' Auntie Shirley was in the kitchen, cook'n someth'n that smelled really good! An' my Daddy an' Mama was home together for the first time! It was also the first time Jimmy been in my house, too. An' he stayed for dinner!

While we was eat'n dinner, Daddy say that he was go'n back to Mobile in the morn'n for a couple days to take care of some things with his truck'n business. He say he would be back early on Thursday morn'n to meet the attorney, an' then he would go downtown to Sheriff Gilmore's office an' turn himself in. I was kinda sad, 'cause I didn't want Daddy to go. But Mama say, "Baby, it's gonna be okay, your daddy will be back. He's home now, baby."

Hear'n Mama say that brought joy to my body. Mama say'n daddy was home now! I don't know exactly what that mean, but I was happy! Before I went to bed, I asked Mama if we could go an' see Mo at the hospital tomorrow after school. I wanted to tell Mo 'bout my daddy be'n home now! Mama say okay.

On Tuesday, Daddy left earlier that morn'n go'n back to Mobile. After school me an' Mama went to see Mo—he was so happy to see me. They had moved him to another room though. Ms. Rosie Mae say to Mama that the doctor told her all signs indicated Mo's body had completely accepted the new kidney—an' he was recover'n very well—so they moved him.

While Mama an' Ms. Rosie Mae was talk'n, I told Mo all 'bout my daddy be'n home now. Well, he's live'n at Uncle Wayne an' Auntie Shirley's house, but Mo was so happy for me still. He thanked me so much for find'n his daddy, an' his new little sisters!

Before me an' Mama left the hospital, we went to Mo's daddy's room to see how he was do'n, too. I wanted to thank him again for help'n Mo—an' give'n him a new kidney—an' for help'n me to find my daddy. Then we left go'n back home. Mama smiled an' say how proud she was of me! She say that I was lett'n God work through me to show His miracles an' love.

Thomas returned to Greene County early Thursday morning after organizing his trucking business to operate in his absence by scaling back to two trucks hauling from the docks instead of three. Sergeant Yoholo was overjoyed that Thomas was "making right the crooked path he had already traveled." Now his path would open doors to new possibilities. He felt Thomas was now being led by his natural inner spirit—the way of the Native American.

Thomas met Virginia, Pastor Winewright, Jimmy and attorney Earl P. Gilliam at the First Baptist Church, in Pastor Winewright's office. After much discussion, Attorney Gilliam laid out what he expected to be the outcome from

Thomas turning himself in to Sheriff Gilmore and pleading self-defense to the District Attorney in the death of Pastor Lee. He said that Thomas would be arrested and booked, and that Jimmy would immediately post a bail bond for Thomas's release. They hoped Thomas would be released before the end of the day. Then they all left to go to Sheriff Gilmore's office in downtown Eutaw.

When they arrived at Sheriff Gilmore's office, District Attorney Gregory Session was there, waiting. Attorney Gilliam had phoned the sheriff and informed him of what was going to happen and to give him the approximate time Thomas would arrive at his office.

Thomas, Attorney Gilliam, Sheriff Gilmore and District Attorney Session went into a separate room, leaving Virginia, Pastor Winewright and Jimmy to wait in the sheriff's office. After about two hours of questioning by District Attorney Session and negotiating by Attorney Gilliam, Thomas was temporarily booked on a charge of "voluntary manslaughter" for the death of Pastor James Robert Lee. Attorney Gilliam argued that no charges should be filed against Thomas because it was a case of self-defense, a trial would be a waste of taxpayers' time and money, and his client would be vindicated in a trial.

District Attorney Session telephoned the court and had Thomas scheduled for arraignment the next morning, Friday, at eleven o'clock in the morning in Superior Court Judge William Wallace's courtroom.

Bail was set at two hundred and fifty thousand dollars, for which Jimmy Lee posted a bond. Thomas was free but told not to leave the state of Alabama while he was out on bail or his bond would be forfeited, and he would be arrested immediately. Attorney Gilliam had negotiated for the allowance of Thomas to travel within the state of Alabama, because his official residence was still in Mobile, and it would allow Thomas to continue operating his sixteen-wheeler tractor trailer truck for the port of Mobile, Alabama.

When I got home from school on Thursday, I was hope'n Daddy would be there, 'cause Mama say that Daddy was come'n back from Mobile today. But there was no one home when I got there. Mama left me a note tell'n me to go to Uncle Wayne an' Auntie Shirley's house, 'cause she might be home late. So I rode my bike over to their house.

I wasn't disappointed 'cause I always like go'n over to their house. It always feel like a party is go'n on over there, people come'n by, an' auntie always be'n in the kitchen, cook'n someth'n good. It wasn't long after I got over there, Mama an' Daddy come over. I was a little surprised how everybody was so excited to see Mama an' Daddy. Then I found out later Daddy had been arrested—well, he turned himself in—by Sheriff Gilmore. Nobody was sure if he would get out of jail today, but they did let him out.

We stayed over Uncle Wayne an' Auntie Shirley's for dinner, Daddy tell'n them all 'bout what happened today at the sheriff's office. He say he had to go back to court, in town, tomorrow morn'n with Attorney Gilliam to plead not guilty to the district attorney charges before the judge. He say the judge was gonna set a trial date an' some other stuff. Mama sent me out the room when Daddy started explain'n what all that means.

When it was time to go home, Mama give me the best news. She say Daddy was move'n back to Greene County. He was gonna move in with Uncle Wayne an' Auntie Shirley. But we was gonna spend a lot of time together, gett'n to know each other as a family. An' one day, we would live together as a family!

Now it feel like my dream is finally gonna come true. I'm gonna have a whole family, just like Mo's little sisters have—an' now Mo!

On the way home, Mama also told me that, while Daddy is now back home in Greene County, he is gonna be go'n to court 'bout someth'n bad that happened a long time ago. She explained that when Daddy starts go'n to court, the news 'bout Daddy's court trial is gonna have people talk'n 'bout it all around town. Mama say I am not to worry 'bout the things I might hear, 'cause everyth'n is gonna be alright. My daddy is gonna get his freedom back from what had happened to him, she say, "because one day, America is gonna be fair for all people."

I didn't really understand what Mama was say'n, but she was so calm tell'n me 'bout it. I just started think'n 'bout Daddy be'n home now. But then I remembered what Jimmy told me when we was drive'n to Mobile. He told me what had happened that day when him an' Daddy saw that boy be'n lynched.

So I started think'n, maybe that's the trouble Mama was talk'n 'bout happened a long time ago, an' that's why Daddy had to go to court so he could get his freedom back? Maybe from have'n to think 'bout it by himself— like Jimmy say—or maybe 'cause Daddy didn't tell nobody?

Before go'n to bed, I asked Mama if we could go an' see Mo again at the hospital tomorrow after school. She say yes.

This had to be the best Friday morn'n I ever had, 'cause when I woke up an' went into the kitchen, Mama an' Daddy was both sitt'n at the kitchen table talk'n. Both of them was greet'n me with a big smile an' good morn'n! Yep, this was the best morn'n ever!

Daddy had walked over from Uncle Wayne's. When I get ready to leave for school, Daddy did someth'n I will always remember—Daddy walked me to school! I would always dream—when I was little an' I would see other little girls walk'n to school with their daddies—that one day I would walk to school with my daddy, too. No, I'll never forget this day!

But while at school, it feel like the longest day, 'cause I couldn't wait for school to end so I could see Mo—when me an' Mama go to the hospital—an' maybe Daddy would go with us? 'Cause I can tell Mo that my daddy is really, really home—well, still kinda—'cause Uncle Wayne an' Auntie Shirley live so close by that Daddy can walk over. But now I have a whole family, too!

Downtown Eutaw
(Courthouse—Friday, October 12, 1979)

Later that morning, Thomas, Virginia, Pastor Winewright, Jimmy and Wayne met Attorney Gilliam at the courthouse in Eutaw for Thomas's arraignment. Presiding Judge William Wallace read the charge brought by District Attorney Gregory Session of "voluntary manslaughter" in the death of James Robert Lee, Sr. Judge Wallace asked Thomas if he understood the charge and how did he plead? Thomas answered, "Yes, your Honor, I understand the charge and I plead not guilty!" Judge Wallace then set a court date for

Monday, January fifteenth, 1980 at nine o'clock a.m.

As it turned out, Judge Wallace was related to the governor of Alabama, Governor George Wallace and District Attorney Session's name was on a shortlist of candidates being considered for appointment to the position of Alabama state attorney general by the governor. Thomas's case, unbeknownst to him or Attorney Gilliam, was partly politically motivated. A conviction of Thomas before the June 1980 state elections—where the current attorney general was sure to win the United States senate seat—could give the district attorney the visibility needed to secure the appointment of the vacated state attorney general position.

Eutaw General Hospital

I was so happy to see Mo an' tell him 'bout my daddy be'n home. I didn't realize at first that Mo wasn't sitt'n in his bed when we walked in—he was sitt'n in a chair at the window, talk'n to his daddy. Mr. Wright was sitt'n next to him! Jacqueline an' Patricia was also there in Mo's room.

Mama an' Mr. Wright was talk'n when Mo's mama an' Ms. Johnnie Mae come in the room with Dr. Wynn. They all started talk'n an' ask'n Dr. Wynn questions 'bout Mo's condition.

But I wasn't listen'n to them 'cause Mo come an'

get in his bed, an' I was so excited tell'n Mo 'bout my daddy be'n home—well, kinda home. I told Mo that my daddy was gonna be live'n with Uncle Wayne an' Auntie Shirley for a while, but Mama say he's gonna come home to live with us one day—maybe soon. An' I told Mo 'bout how my daddy walked me to school! Mo was so happy for me—we was happy for each other— Mo had his daddy, an' I had my daddy, too!

Just then I thought, then I say to Mo, "You an' your daddy will always be together now, 'cause you have one of his kidneys inside your body."

Like when Mama gave me that necklace chain an' tag with my daddy's name on it—an' she say that as long as I wear it, my daddy would be right there with me, next to my heart. I started wonder'n, how close is Mo's new kidney to his heart? Then I told Mo his new kidney must be closer to his heart than my necklace chain is to mine.

Dr. Wynn come over to the bedside where Mo an' me was an' he sat down. Ms. Rosie Mae, Mama, Ms. Johnnie Mae, Mr. Wright an' Mo's little sisters all come over an' stood around Mo's bed. Dr. Wynn say to Mo, "How would you like to go home, young man?"

Mo's eyes get all big—he was excited. He say, "Yes! Yes, I want to go home!" Dr. Wynn turned to Ms. Rosie Mae an' say that Mo was be'n released to go home the next morn'n. Everybody get excited with Mo, when Dr.

Wynn say that!

Mo asked Dr. Wynn if he could go back to school on Monday, now that he was go'n home? Mo's mama started laugh'n. She say that Mo has never been this excited to go to school since he was in kindergarten! Dr. Wynn say he wanted Mo to stay home from school for one more week. He wanted Mo's body to gain more strength, an' to let his body strengthen its immune system first before go'n back to school.

On the way home, Mama told me that Mo's daddy was be'n released from the hospital to go home to his family tomorrow, too. She say, "Baby, God has performed a miracle for both our families—by bring'n Mo's daddy back into his life, an' you, baby, now you have your daddy here in your life, too. Only God could have used you like that, baby—to do His will."

Mo come home on Saturday, so when I finished all my chores, I asked Mama if I could ride my bike over to Mo's house an' stay over there all day visit'n with him? Mama looked at me with a funny smile an' say, "Olivia Jones, yes you can, but you go straight to Mo's house an' that's all, okay?"

I say, "Yes, Mama."

Me an' Mo spent the whole weekend—Saturday an'

Sunday—play'n Scrabble, cards an' some other games. Mo was happy to be back home an' I'm happy we can hang out together again.

One and a half months later

Thanksgiv'n was the best ever. We all gathered over Uncle Wayne an' Auntie Shirley's. It was my first Thanksgiv'n with my daddy home. I saw my daddy almost every day dur'n Thanksgiv'n an' winter break from school. I would go by Uncle Wayne's an' Auntie Shirley's or Daddy would come by an' visit Mama an' me. Mama an' Daddy started date'n—well, kinda— 'cause they took me everywhere with them...to the movie...down to the lake...we even drove to Selma take'n Mo to visit with his daddy an' his family.

The most fun though, was when Mama let me go to work with daddy an' I rode in his sixteen-wheeler truck that day. Daddy had a load of paper product he was take'n from Tuscaloosa to Mobile, Alabama shipyard. It was so different from when I was with Jimmy drive'n to Mobile that first time to find my daddy. I was think'n so much 'bout find'n my daddy that I didn't really see how beautiful the land in Alabama was. But sitt'n in my daddy's truck—it's so high I can see so much now—I

115

really enjoyed see'n Alabama. But just be'n with my daddy I enjoyed the most.

When school started back, I wasn't that happy 'cause I was have'n so much fun be'n with Mama an' Daddy, an' Mo, too. We was back to "old Mo an' me," ride'n our bikes an' have'n fun play'n. Mo's mama say that the doctors was amazed 'bout how well Mo was recover'n so fast after his surgery. Mama say, "That's how God works!"

Well, we only been back at school for one week after winter break. When I get home, Mama an' Daddy was there an' they both seemed upset. At first I thought I did someth'n wrong, but then I found out they was upset 'cause what was in the local newspaper. There was a picture in the paper of my daddy—a picture me an' Mama never seen before. Daddy was in his Army uniform an' another Army soldier was pinn'n that medal me an' Mo found in the backyard on Daddy's shirt. Below the picture it say, "Negro soldier dishonors country with the brutal death of Eutaw's beloved local pastor."

Mama was shocked how the paper made my daddy seem like a murderer—a really bad person. Mama an' Daddy sat me down an' told me 'bout what happened to Pastor Lee on the night that Daddy first come back home from the Army. Daddy explained how he should have stayed an' reported to the sheriff what had happened, but he was afraid the sheriff wouldn't believe him an' that they might have lynched Daddy that night.

Daddy was afraid 'cause Sheriff Joe Clark was a member of the Klan with Pastor Lee. Daddy say him an' Jimmy saw the sheriff and Pastor Lee lynch a boy long time ago. Then Mama say, "Baby, this is the trouble I was talk'n 'bout. That's why your daddy has to go to court to tell the judge the truth 'bout what happened to Pastor Lee—Jimmy's daddy—that night!"

I asked Mama was Daddy gonna have to go to jail? Then I started cry'n 'cause I was think'n 'bout my daddy have'n to leave us again! Mama say, "No baby, Daddy has a good lawyer an' he is go'n to fight to get his freedom from all this." Daddy smiled an' give me a big hug. Mama joined in—group hug!

Sunday, the night before Daddy had to go to court for the trial, I heard Daddy an' Mama talk'n 'bout it in the kitchen. Mama was say'n that the district attorney was out to get Daddy, 'cause she had heard he wanted the governor to appoint him to a bigger job as the state attorney general—an' winn'n this trial against Daddy would help him get that bigger job. Mama say that she was really concerned that Daddy might not get a fair trial. Then I heard Mama pray'n to God to help make

America fair for all people—not just White people—an'
especially fair for my daddy!

Downtown Eutaw
(Courthouse—Monday, January 15, 1980)

Monday morning, when Thomas and Virginia arrived
at the courthouse, they were surprised at all the news
reporters and the people that were there, from all over. Once
inside, they were greeted by Attorney Gilliam who then
introduced two attorneys, Ms. Trapp and Mr. Carothers,
from the National Association for the Advancement of
Colored People (NAACP) Legal Defense Fund. They had
joined Attorney Gilliam in Thomas's defense and had been
working with him over the past three weeks going over
case law preparing for trial. They were determined to help
Attorney Gilliam present a winning strategy for the case.

Thomas was a war hero, decorated by the United States
Army with the Medal of Honor! That's the character they
were planning to present to the jury. Unfortunately, the final
jury selection did not accurately represent the community
of Eutaw (which was sixty-six percent Black people) or
Thomas's peers. There were eleven Whites and only one
Black person selected on the jury, and only two jurors were
women. The local newspaper ran articles painting Pastor

Lee as a saint and Thomas as a dishonored soldier.

Because of the controversial atmosphere the case had created—in and around Eutaw—Attorney Gilliam petitioned the court, the week before the trial, to move the case to a less hostile neutral court in another city. Judge Wallace struck down the petition, and said the trial would remain in his courtroom, starting Monday morning. The first two days in court were spent on jury selection. The evidence part of the trial began on the third day.

Wednesday morning—first week of trial

The trial proceeded at a fast pace. Neither side had any hard physical evidence to back their case—both relied on circumstantial evidence.

Thomas's defense mainly revolved around Thomas's testimony of self-defense, and the prosecution's case relied on character witnesses and a statement made by Ms. Lee during the initial investigation at her home by then Sheriff Clark. She had stated that she heard Pastor Lee talking to someone before a little commotion in the house, causing her to go downstairs, where she found Pastor Lee lying on the floor.

District Attorney Session made his opening statement for the prosecution. The district attorney said that he was going to prove that Thomas had killed Pastor James Robert Lee, Sr. out of a rage when Pastor Lee confronted

Thomas for illegally trespassing in his home—and that the story Thomas has told of Pastor Lee being at some remote incident ten or twenty years earlier was without merit or fact.

The district attorney was working to create the narrative for Thomas's testimony before Thomas had a chance to tell his story. The district attorney took what Thomas had previously stated and twisted it for the jury as though Thomas had mistakenly thought he had witnessed Pastor Lee participate in a crime more than a decade earlier. He contended that, when presented with the truth from Pastor Lee on that fateful night—the truth that Pastor Lee was not present on the night that had been in question—Thomas became enraged and attacked Pastor Lee, choking him to death.

Attorney Gilliam made his opening statement. He stated that his team would present to the jury the true character of Thomas—a war hero decorated for his bravery, integrity and commitment to honor and sacrifice for his fellow soldiers and his country. They were going to prove that Thomas was a man of great integrity and that his testimony would be the truth, the whole truth and nothing less!

The prosecution presented its case to the jury over the next four business days (Wednesday through Monday). Then the prosecution rested (finished presenting its case) on Monday afternoon, January twenty-first, 1980. At that time Attorney Gilliam made a motion to the court to dismiss the case "with prejudice" because he believed that the district attorney failed to present a single thread of evidence to prove its case.

Judge Wallace quickly denied the "motion to dismiss" and adjourned the court until the next morning, Tuesday, when the defense was to present its case to the jury through direct examination and witnesses.

All week long, seem like all everybody was talk'n 'bout was Daddy's trial. Daddy had been in court every day. When Sunday come, Daddy went to church with Mama an' me. Pastor Winewright had the whole church pray'n for Daddy. They's pray'n for truth an' justice to win in Daddy's court trial—an' that the court would find Daddy not guilty an' set him free from all this terrible burden. Me an' Mama been pray'n every night for Daddy. Mo been pray'n, too.

Tuesday, Attorney Gilliam and his team began to present their case to the jury, but they soon found out how difficult the district attorney was going to make it for them to present the strategy they had planned. The district attorney objected at almost every turn, and when he objected to the testimony that Jimmy Lee was to give, the judge called them up to his bench for discussion. Attorney Gilliam argued that Jimmy was there to corroborate the testimony he had given in his deposition which the court had as exhibit #377915.

Then the judge said that he would rule by the following morning as to the extent to which Jimmy could testify, and he adjourned the court for the day.

When Mama come to pick me up from Uncle Wayne an' Auntie Shirley's, she was really worried. She told Uncle Wayne an' Auntie Shirley that she feel like the judge wasn't gonna let Jimmy testify for Daddy's defense by tell'n the court 'bout what him an' Daddy saw that night when they saw Pastor Lee at that lynch'n of that boy, Tony. She say that was an important part of Daddy's defense case. Now she was really worried that my daddy's trial wasn't gonna be fair without Jimmy be'n able to testify.

Wednesday morning, Judge Wallace ruled that Jimmy could testify but only on the specific matter before the court, and nothing more. He said that Jimmy could not talk about what he did or did not see at a lynching or about anything else that was not before his court. In the judge's ruling he stated that Pastor James Robert Lee, Sr. was not on trial in his court, but Thomas Jefferson Jones was!

Attorney Gilliam asked the court for an early recess to allow him to bring in a replacement witness for the defense. The judge granted recess and to reconvene Thursday at one o'clock p.m., giving the defense twenty-four hours to regroup.

Attorney Gilliam had previously deposed Sergeant Ernie Natan Yoholo and had told him that he might need his testimony as a character witness on Thomas's behalf. So, when he recontacted Sergeant Yoholo and asked if he could come up to Eutaw and testify on Thursday afternoon, he said he was honored to do so and would be there by noon.

Thursday afternoon, Sergeant Yoholo testified on behalf of Thomas's character as a soldier and as a friend. However, the defense team had to make another change to their strategy. Without Jimmy's testimony, the defense needed to bring into the record Thomas's account of what happened the night he and Jimmy saw Pastor Lee at the lynching.

They called Thomas to the witness stand to testify on his own behalf. They had hoped that with a strong testimony from Jimmy—the Pastor's son—Thomas would not need to take the witness stand himself. Attorney Gilliam didn't want Thomas before the jury admitting that he angrily confronted Pastor Lee, and subsequently choked the pastor unconscious.

After Thomas's testimony and cross examination by the district attorney, the defense rested. Thomas's attorneys were finished presenting their case. Judge Wallace adjourned the court until Friday morning to hear closing arguments. He summoned both lead attorneys Gilliam and Session to his chambers for a settlement conference on jury instructions.

On Friday of the second week of the trial, the prosecution presented its closing arguments to the jury, making its case for Pastor Lee as a "most beloved husband, father, minister and righteous citizen of his community."

Then the defense presented their closing arguments, making the case for Thomas as a "dedicated and honorable soldier with a high degree of integrity and honesty...and his acts on the night in question were purely in self-defense from an enraged attacker, Pastor Lee."

After both closing statements, Judge Wallace gave the jury instructions. The judge instructed the jury about what law to apply to the case and how to carry out its duties. The jury was then set to start its deliberations on Monday morning, January twenty-eighth, 1980.

On Friday, after the court adjourned, everybody—

Thomas, Virginia, Attorneys Gilliam, Carothers and Trapp, Pastor Winewright and Jimmy—left the courthouse to go and have dinner at Wayne and Shirley's home.

There was a great sense of relief that the trial was over, however, there was also much anxiousness about the makeup of the jurors (one Black woman, one White woman and ten White men) and what might be their subsequent verdict.

I was happy—kinda—'cause Mama an' Daddy was both here at Uncle Wayne an' Auntie Shirley's home together. But from what I understood from everybody talk'n 'bout Daddy's trial, Daddy could—maybe—go to jail if the jury don't find him innocent. We stayed over Auntie Shirley an' Uncle Wayne's a long time. I fell asleep. Daddy woke me up when Mama was ready to go home. I told Mama I hope Daddy could come home with us tonight. Mama just say, "Soon, baby, we'll talk 'bout it in the morn'n."

Saturday morn'n when I woke up an' went in the kitchen, Mama an' Daddy was sitt'n at the table, an' Mama made my favorite breakfast—grits, eggs, bacon an' waffles! We all sat an' had breakfast together—as a family! Mama say, "Olivia, we have some news to tell you."

My eyes get really big, 'cause I'm think'n the jury made up they mind an' had a decision 'bout Daddy's trial. But Mama say, "Baby, your daddy an' I are go'n to get married again. We are ready to be a whole family together!" I was so excited, I just cried happy tears. Mama an' Daddy hugged me.

Then Mama say, "Your daddy an' me decided to have a wedd'n ceremony at the church in the springtime— Saturday, May third—in just three months." She say I was gonna be in the wedd'n, too! Mama say, on that day, Daddy would be all the way home to stay for good. Our lives would start all over in the same house together as the new Jones family!

I was so excited, I had to tell my best friend, Mo. Mama an' Daddy gonna get married again, an' I'm gonna be in it! I did my chores really fast an' I asked Mama if I could go over to Mo's house. She say okay. Me an' Mo spent the whole day together. He was so happy 'bout the news I tell him 'bout Mama an' Daddy gett'n married.

Sunday morn'n, Daddy come over. Me an' Mama an'

Daddy went to church together. Me, Mo an' Champ met at Sunday school. I was so excited to tell Mo on Saturday that Mama an' Daddy was gett'n married again, that I forget to tell him they's gett'n married right here in our church, where everybody could see us as a family in the wedd'n. Mo thought that was really cool, me be'n in the wedd'n with both my parents.

Then he asked how many kids you think ever been in their own mama an' daddy's wedd'n before? 'Cause I was gonna be the first one he ever heard of—me, too! Mama also say that I can help decorate the church when it's time for the wedd'n.

Downtown Eutaw
(Courthouse)

Monday, the jury began deliberations on the trial. Judge Wallace reminded the jury of the law they were to apply to Thomas's case. The jury deliberated all day Monday, and again on Tuesday, adjourning both days without reaching a unanimous verdict.

Wednesday afternoon, the jury foreman sent a letter to Judge Wallace. It read:

Dear Judge Wallace,

I believe we the jury have reached a deadlock. We have gone over very thoroughly all the known aspects of the case with the utmost care to only apply the law, as we were instructed, and deliberating with open minds. Yet we are unable to reach a unanimous decision. After several straw votes, we are at a ten–one–one split. I am not sure what to do next. We are requesting clarification and direction.
Signed, Juror #1

The jury had taken several votes and remained split ten to one to one (ten to convict, one to acquit and one undecided). Judge Wallace called the jury and both lead attorneys back to the courtroom where he gave them additional instruction. He admonished the jury that they were to deliberate on the facts of the case only. And though Mr. Jones made testimony about the character of Pastor Lee and his version of the truth, it was just that, his version of the truth. He implied that Thomas was lying.

At that point Attorney Gilliam objected to the judge's instruction, stating that it was bias against his client. Judge Wallace acknowledged his objection, then proceeded to instruct the jury to go back and deliberate another twenty-four hours and take a final vote on Friday afternoon.

Word had gotten out that the trial was going to end in a hung jury. The newspaper, radio and local television news talk of a pending hung jury had the whole town buzzing with conversation about what people thought was going to happen with the trial.

Attorney Gilliam an' Daddy was at my house when I get home from school. They was talk'n 'bout Daddy's trial. From what I understood, Attorney Gilliam was want'n the jury to be hung. He say that he would then request to the judge to dismiss Daddy's case.

On Friday afternoon, February first, Judge Wallace called all parties back to court. The jury had rendered its decision. With all parties present, court was back in session. Judge Wallace asked if the jury had rendered its decision. The foreman stood, affirmed that it had, then handed the bailiff a handwritten note. Judge Wallace asked the bailiff to read the jury's verdict to the court.

"We the jury find the defendant, Thomas Jefferson Jones, guilty on one count of voluntary manslaughter."

Thomas, Attorney Gilliam and his team were taken aback with the verdict, especially in light of the news circulating that the jury was hung, ten–one–one—so what happened? Prior to the verdict being read, Attorney Gilliam anticipated a hung jury, at which point he was prepared to file a motion to acquit his client. He was stunned!

Judge Wallace set a hearing for sentencing on Monday, March third at nine o'clock a.m. In the meantime, Thomas remained free on the two hundred and fifty thousand dollars original bond.

The city of Eutaw was really buzzing with both excitement and despair with anger. Emotions were split along racial lines. White citizens believed that the verdict was right, and that Pastor Lee was an honest, righteous man. Conversely, the Black community had its long-held suspicions about Pastor Lee's Klan associations. They were angry with the verdict.

Mama an' me was at Uncle Wayne an' Auntie Shirley's on Friday night after the jury say Daddy was guilty. Mama an' Daddy told Uncle Wayne an' Auntie that Daddy was gonna appeal the jury verdict. Daddy say he's gonna ask a higher court judge to change the jury's decision—to not guilty—'cause it was self-defense. Daddy say that he was told he would have to get another attorney to file for the appeal. There was someth'n special 'bout file'n the appeal an' that Attorney Gilliam would need help from the NAACP legal defense team. We heard they was already on alert an' provide'n support to Attorney Gilliam.

When we get home, Mama say Daddy is gonna fight his case all the way to the Supreme Court—the highest court in America—if he has to! Then she say, "Don't worry, baby, your daddy ain't go'n nowhere, 'cause we a family now. God brought us back together, an' no judge or no jury gonna take that from us!"

After that night, everyth'n seemed kinda normal to me again. I saw Daddy almost every day. He would come an' walk me to school in the morn'n, except when he was drive'n his big truck an' trailer across Alabama. Nobody was talk'n 'bout Daddy's trial anymore. We was all talk'n 'bout Mama an' Daddy gett'n married in May.

But then one night, 'bout a couple weeks later (around February eighteenth) Daddy, Jimmy, Attorney Gilliam an' Uncle Wayne come to the house to talk to Mama 'bout someth'n really important 'bout Daddy's trial. Jimmy told Mama what he had already told Daddy, Attorney Gilliam an' Uncle Wayne. He told Mama 'bout a book his mom gave him a couple days after the jury's verdict. Jimmy's mom told him she had planned for him to get the book after she passed away.

Jimmy's mother had fallen ill just a few months after his father's death, so Jimmy returned home. He had been his mother's primary caregiver ever since, along with help from Diane, a middle-aged widow from Pastor Lee's church family. Jimmy's mother's poor health was the only reason he had returned to Greene County. He hadn't even traveled back home to Greene County for his father's funeral. But when his mom took ill, he came home, and remained.

Jimmy said that his mom had followed the trial with great interest, asking him regularly how the trial was progressing. But after he told her that the jury's verdict was guilty of manslaughter, she moaned. He said she was visibly upset. But she didn't say anything else to him. Two days later she gave him the book he had in his hand, which turned out to be her diary she had kept ever since Jimmy's birth.

She said, "Son you need to read this book now. You'll understand why later. It may answer some of the unanswered questions that you have about yourself and your relationship with your father."

Jimmy said that he didn't understand, and he was a little afraid of what he might find, so he didn't really want to read what was in it. He just carried it around with him for a while. But the other day, while he was sitting at the lake, he opened it and started thumbing through. At times it was overwhelming, because it made him relive in his mind some unpleasant moments in the past.

He read about the time his father had taken him to a Young White Christian Leadership meeting. His mom wrote in her diary that it was actually a Ku Klux Klan rally. The revelations were astonishing, including the argument that his mom had with his father the night he took Jimmy (five years of age) to the Klan rally disguised as a Christian Leadership meeting. His mom had threatened to take Jimmy, and leave his father, if he ever tried to take Jimmy to another of those Klan rallies or anywhere near a Klansman!

Jimmy was emotionally floored when he read about that encounter. He remembered how frightened he was that night as a little boy, and how he became fearful of his father—he began to stutter as a child after that. He was shaken just talking about it.

But then he said, as he started really reading further through her diary, he discovered why he thinks his mom was so upset by the jury's verdict.

She wrote that on the night of his father's death, his mom found the Army patch that was torn from Thomas's jacket, and the fireplace log iron on the floor pushed behind the sofa. She gathered both items and put them in a plastic bag, then placed the bag in the downstairs closet.

She also wrote that there was blood all over both items, but Jimmy's father wasn't cut or bleeding at the time of his death. So, the blood must have been someone else's. Three days after his father's death, Sheriff Clark came by the house asking questions about the night of his death, at which time she gave him the bag with both the patch and the fireplace iron inside.

Jimmy (rhetorically) questioned Thomas and Attorney Gilliam, "Why...? This is the evidence that neither the DA nor Attorney Gilliam had, but it should have been made available by the sheriff's office, or the DA's office—whoever has it!"

Jimmy realized that Attorney Gilliam was put at an unfair disadvantage to argue Thomas's case of self-defense without this crucial evidence. It clearly showed—in Jimmy's mind—that Thomas was telling the truth about self-defense, and that the sheriff had the evidence all along!

Jimmy asked Attorney Gilliam if this evidence could be subpoenaed, and—if recovered—could it be used in Thomas's appeal? Attorney Gilliam stated that the answer was not so simple. Generally, it is not allowed to introduce new or additional evidence at the appeal. Only evidence submitted in the previous proceedings is admissible. However, new evidence may be introduced with leave (permission) from the division hearing the appeal—three judges in this case.

Gilliam went on to say, "Our challenge with this appeal is the fact that the three judges appointed to the courts division, that would be hearing our appeal, were all appointed by Governor George Wallace." He continued, "Our strategy may have to be: let's fail fast...meaning, get through this level of appeal as quickly as possible, aiming for appeal to the state Supreme Court, and if necessary, then the highest court, the United States Supreme Court, for relief."

Jimmy gave Attorney Gilliam the diary, hoping that somehow it could be used to help get Thomas free from the jury's guilty verdict of voluntary manslaughter. After a little more conversation, Attorney Gilliam explained that if such evidence existed, it would be considered "exculpatory evidence," meaning it's evidence favorable to the defendant in a criminal trial that exonerates (clears/acquits) or tends to exonerate the defendant of guilt—in this case, Thomas.

They all agreed to give Attorney Gilliam some time to evaluate the diary with his team of attorneys from the NAACP Legal Defense Fund, and plan the next steps to take with this new information. They then all departed except Thomas. He and Virginia talked pretty much throughout the night.

The next morn'n, I was surprised to see Daddy was already at our house, 'cause when I went to bed it was late an' he was still here, an' now he was in the kitchen where Mama was make'n breakfast. After we ate, Daddy walked me to school. He say that I was gonna be the most beautiful flower girl ever to be in a wedd'n!

I told Daddy that I could barely wait for that day to come, 'cause I want to wake up every morn'n an' see his smile'n eyes. He smiled an' say, "We only have ten more weeks to wait!"

Well, time really did fly by. The next eight weeks, no one was talk'n 'bout Daddy's trial anymore. I didn't even hear Mama or Daddy talk'n 'bout it. Except I did hear Daddy talk'n to that attorney from the NAACP, someth'n 'bout lose'n the appeal. Daddy didn't seem mad or anyth'n. He say to him, "Well, we will appeal to the state Supreme Court, and even higher than that if we have to—to get justice!" Then Daddy hung up the phone.

Mama picked blue an' gold to be the colors for her an' Daddy's wedd'n. She showed me the material an' it was so beautiful. I was gonna have blue an' gold ribbons in my hair with a beautiful light blue dress, gold socks an' blue shoes.

A week before the wedd'n Daddy an' Uncle Wayne come to the house 'cause they had some information 'bout Daddy's trial he wanted to tell Mama. Daddy say the attorneys immediately filed an appeal to the Alabama Supreme Court after the first appeal was rejected by the three-judge panel of appeal. He say the attorneys was hope'n to have an answer back soon from the appeal to the state Supreme Court, if it was gonna consider the appeal. They say that if the state refused to consider the appeal, that was good, 'cause that would then allow Daddy's attorneys to appeal to the United States Supreme Court—the highest court in America!

They also say that Daddy's attorneys was work'n hard at the same time to get a federal judge to issue a subpoena to the Eutaw district attorney an' the Eutaw sheriff's office for the evidence log book an' the evidence Jimmy's mom gave to Sheriff Clark three days after Jimmy's dad's death.

After they told Mama all 'bout it, Uncle Wayne left go'n back home, but Daddy stayed over talk'n with Mama. She was upset an' nervous 'bout all that appeal stuff that was still go'n on with the wedd'n just a week away.

When I woke up in the morn'n, Daddy was sitt'n at the breakfast table still talk'n to Mama—an' my breakfast was on the table wait'n on me! Daddy walked me to school. He say he had to go to Mobile for a few days an' that he would be back on Thursday, two days before the wedd'n. Daddy hugged me an' say again that I was gonna be the most beautiful flower girl that anyone ever seen!

Sho-enough, Daddy was back home on Thursday even'n. I was at the church with Mama an' some of the ladies from church. We was clean'n up an' decorate'n for the wedd'n. Daddy told Mama he had some good news an' some good news! Then he laughed!

He say, "Virginia, the Alabama Supreme Court refused to consider the appeal." Mama was look'n puzzled. Then Daddy say to Mama, "Remember, honey, that's what we wanted. It clears the way for us to appeal to the United States Supreme Court!" Mama's eyes get all big—she looked like she was scared an' happy at the same time.

Daddy say, "The other good news is the NAACP attorneys have gotten a federal judge to issue a subpoena for the evidence that Jimmy's mom gave to the sheriff. The subpoena goes out to the sheriff and district attorney's offices on Monday!" Mama didn't seem as happy as Daddy—she had so much on her mind—with decorate'n the church an' all the wedd'n stuff, but she was happy—kinda.

On Friday, the night before the wedd'n, I stayed over Uncle Wayne an' Auntie Shirley's house so when I saw Mama on Saturday all dressed for the wedd'n, she was so beautiful—like an angel from heaven! I just started cry'n, but Mama she stopped me say'n, "No, babe, you'll make me cry, too, an' that would mess up all my makeup." So I stopped myself.

There was so many people in the church, all smile'n an' happy for Mama gett'n married to Daddy. It seemed like a really far walk for me to drop flowers all the way from the back of the church to the altar where Pastor Winewright was stand'n. I was a little nervous, but when I started walk'n, I was more happy that I was the flower girl in Mama an' Daddy's wedd'n, I just forget 'bout be'n nervous! I looked over at Mo an' he was so happy for me an' Mama. He was sitt'n there with his whole new family—Jacqueline, Patricia, Ms. Johnnie Mae Wright, Ms. Rosie Mae Wright an' his daddy!

When Mama come down the aisle, she was as radiant as the sun, a glow shine'n from her smile reflect'n all around the church. I think God musta been smile'n, too, 'cause when Daddy took Mama's hand it felt magical. I can't explain it, but I think everyth'n everywhere just stopped! An' everybody in the church was hold'n their breath anticipate'n the magic. The love that God gave my Mama an' Daddy!

I don't remember what all they say to each other, but when Mama say, "I do," an' Pastor Winewright told Daddy he could kiss Mama, everybody in the church started clapp'n an' shout'n an' some was dance'n— shout'n, "Hallelujah! Hallelujah!"

I heard a man say'n to the lady with him that Mama was "...God's kinda girl—she waited on God to deliver her man back home to her an' their little girl. Ain't God good!" In my mind I'm scream'n—my Mama an' Daddy are married now— we a family for real now!

At the reception, everybody danced an' ate an' danced some more. People even danced with Mama, an' each time they did, they pinned money on Mama's dress. She was loaded with money at the end of the reception.

The next morn'n I woke up before Mama. That almost never happens. When I went in Mama's room, there was Mama an' Daddy, sleep'n in the same bed together! My Daddy's home now! It's also the first time I can remember when me an' Mama didn't go to church on a Sunday morn'n. Then I say to myself, "I gotta idea—I'ma make my Mama an' Daddy breakfast in bed. They gonna wake up smell'n a good-oh breakfast meal—eggs, bacon, grits, biscuits with jam an' orange juice. It's my favorite breakfast meal, well with some waffles!" Before I could finish though, Mama come in the kitchen. She say, "Little girl, what are you up to in here? It sure smells good up in here!" Then we laughed. Mama went an' get Daddy. Breakfast was good. Daddy say it was the best he ever had, 'cept Mama's, of course!

Daddy stayed home from work all the next week. He say it was his honeymoon be'n there away from work in Mobile. Mama seemed so happy an' calm with Daddy be'n home.

When I get home from school on Thursday, everybody

was at my house—Uncle Wayne an' Auntie Shirley, Jimmy, Attorney Gilliam an' the two attorneys from the NAACP—even Pastor Winewright was there. I could tell right away that it was someth'n really important an' it had to do with Daddy's court trial. When I walked in the house, I don't think anyone knew I was there. There was two or three people talk'n all at the same time—it was loud, too. When I spotted Mama in the kitchen behind them, she see me an' smiled an' say, "Come in here, babe..."

I guess Mama could tell from the look on my face that I was confused. So she explained what all the commotion was 'bout. Mama was really calm an' she spoke softly while tell'n me that Daddy's attorneys brought the county sheriff's logbook to the house with them. An' that this book was a very important part of what Daddy's attorneys fought really hard with the Alabama state courts to have released. It has information the attorneys could use to win Daddy's case in court. Then Mama stopped—her face get really serious—an' she say, "That district attorney had that information all along!" It made her mad just think'n 'bout it.

Now I understood why everybody in the other room seemed so serious. The attorney was read'n someth'n in the book to Daddy, an' it had everybody upset 'bout it! Some was say'n it should be a mistrial, others say'n

Daddy should be released immediately from the court verdict. But Daddy's attorney didn't say a word 'bout it. He kept read'n through more pages, then he stopped. He say, although this was a major victory for Daddy's court case, they still need the higher court to agree to hear the case.

That night set the mood for what was to come. Each day after that I would see an' hear more an' more talk 'bout Daddy's trial. Even the newspaper was write'n articles on the front pages 'bout Daddy's trial. They was say'n mean things 'bout Daddy. Mama tried to keep me from see'n or hear'n any of it, but someone was always bring'n it up, just where I could hear it. It wasn't on purpose—people was just talk'n 'bout it everywhere.

The next week Daddy was back go'n to work drive'n his big wheel tractor an' trailer truck—three days in Mobile an' the rest of the time closer to Eutaw.

The next week after that, we was all together again as a family with Uncle Wayne an' Auntie Shirley. We was at they house for the Memorial Day holiday. There was food cook'n in the kitchen—Uncle Wayne was barbecue'n in the front yard—an' us kids was runn'n around outside play'n tag. Both Mo's families was there—his mama an' his daddy, Mo's little sisters an'

142

they mama was all over Uncle Wayne's, too.

Later on when it was gett'n dark we was all in the house. The grownups was in the live'n room play'n cards an' dominoes an' talk'n really loud. All the kids was in the supper room by the kitchen. I heard Daddy explain'n 'bout his court trial. Mama left out the room with us kids an' went an' stood next to Daddy, sitt'n at the card table. Daddy say that his attorneys had filed an application for a "Writ of Habeas Corpus, for constitutional violation, jurisdiction or fundamental defects and post-conviction Habeas"—he used some big words I didn't understand.

Then Daddy say what all that means is, this application filed to the courts was different, unlike the direct appeals before. In this appeal the attorneys could raise new facts an' arguments that were not presented in the first trial court. He say that his case was a good example of a state's district attorney's failure to disclose material—that's called "exculpatory evidence."

Then Daddy explained why the book his attorneys got from their subpoena was so important to his court trial. It was an evidence logbook from the time period of Pastor Lee's death. Daddy say, by itself, it may be all the evidence his attorneys need to clear his conviction an' free him from the trial verdict. But also, it could lead to his attorney gett'n the miss'n hard evidence (the blood-stained Army patch an' the fireplace iron) as well.

When we was on our way home from the party, all my mind was think'n 'bout was Daddy say'n he could be free from that court verdict. I tried to understand what all that meant, what Daddy was say'n—it was too hard, though. I fell fast asleep. When I woke up, I was in my bed an' it was time for school.

Mo an' me was back ride'n our bikes all around, but we couldn't go too far. Mo was still gett'n stronger, but his mama an' the doctor wanted him to take it easy for a while longer. An' Mama gave me that look—you know the one—well, I knew I'd better stay close to home. No more big adventure for me—well, at least not anytime soon.

Summertime seemed to come early this year. We was one week from school lett'n out an' it was already hot! All week Mama an' Daddy was monitor'n an' watch'n the phone. When it rang they'd tell me not to answer it, they would get it.

Attorney Gilliam had told Daddy he had got word, the United States Supreme Court was consider'n hear'n their argument on behalf of Daddy's application for "Writ of Habeas Corpus"—I didn't know what all that means but it must be good.

I never seen Daddy nervous before, so I could tell how

important that phone call he was wait'n on must really be. He didn't want to take a chance lett'n me answer the phone just in case it's 'bout the Supreme Court. Daddy say that Attorney Gilliam thinks that if the Supreme Court agrees to hear his case, they would hear it in the fall session—three or four months away!

Sho-enough, one week later, on my last day of school before summer break, the phone rang an' it was Attorney Gilliam. Mama answered it 'cause Daddy wasn't home from work yet. But I knew what it was 'bout 'cause Mama was just nodd'n her head say'n, "Yes...yes...yes..." an' her body was just shake'n but she was smile'n really big!

When she hung up the phone, she looked at me with that big smile an' say, "Oli, babe, your daddy is gonna be so very happy, 'cause the United States Supreme Court agreed today to hear your daddy's court case!"

146

BIBLIOGRAPHY

These are the writings, authors and iconic figures that informed the "Olivia Jones" story with their lived experiences. I've been so privileged to have spent personal time with each of them (except Ms. Amelia Boynton). Dad and Genise gave me account of their personal stories about Ms. Boynton, and they provided me an original copy of her book. I hope "Olivia's" journey will inspire you to read these books and articles, as well as others, on this important history. I believe we will only get better as a nation to the extent we know our history.

Boynton, Amelia Platts. *Bridge Across Jordan: The Story of the Struggle for Civil Rights in Selma, Alabama.* United States: Carlton Press, 1979.

Fitch, Bob., Stone, Benjamin Lee., Trujillo, Roberto G. *Movements for Change: The Bob Fitch Photography Archive at Stanford.* United States: Stanford University Libraries, (n.d.). (This exhibit catalog contains photographs and information about Thomas Gilmore, the black sheriff of Greene County.)

Jones, Clarence B., Connelly, Stuart. *Behind the Dream: The Making of the Speech that Transformed a Nation.* United

Kingdom: St. Martin's Publishing Group, 2012.

Jones, Clarence B., Engel, Joel. *What Would Martin Say?*. United States: HarperCollins, 2008.

King, Martin Luther. *Letter from the Birmingham Jail*. San Francisco: Harper San Francisco, 1994.

LaFayette, Bernard., Johnson, Kathryn Lee. *In Peace and Freedom: My Journey in Selma*. United States: University Press of Kentucky, 2013.

Vivian, C. T. *Black Power and the American Myth*. United States: Fortress Press, 1970.

Vivian, C. T., Fiffer, Steve. *It's in the Action: Memories of a Nonviolent Warrior*. United States: NewSouth Books, 2021.

Young, Andrew. *An Easy Burden: The Civil Rights Movement and the Transformation of America*. United States: Baylor University Press, 2008.

Young, Andrew., Newman, Harvey. *Andrew Young and the Making of Modern Atlanta*. United States: Mercer University Press, 2016.

Young, Andrew J., Sehgal, Kabir. *Walk in My Shoes:*

Conversations Between a Civil Rights Legend and His Godson on the Journey Ahead. United Kingdom: Palgrave Macmillan, 2010.

GLOSSARY OF LEGAL TERMS
(Google searched)

Arraignment: The first step in criminal proceeding where the defendant is brought in front of the court to hear the charges and enter a plea.

Arrested and Booked: The process typically involves a "booking" process and a bail hearing that determines whether the person arrested may be released pending trial and set the bail amount. Booking creates an official arrest record; arrested suspects who can post bail immediately often can't be released until after the booking process is complete.

Conviction: A formal declaration that someone is guilty of a criminal offense, made by the verdict of a jury or the decision of a judge in a court of law. (Lexico. com)

Dismissed with Prejudice: In the formal legal world, a court case that is dismissed with prejudice means that it is dismissed permanently. A case dismissed with prejudice is over and done with, once and for all, and can't be brought back to court.

Exculpatory Evidence: Exculpatory evidence is evidence favorable to the defendant in a criminal trial that exonerates (clears or acquits) or tends to exonerate the defendant of guilt.

Post a Bond: A bond is posted on a defendant's behalf, usually by a bail bond company, to secure his or her release.

Subpoena: A *subpoena* (pronounced "suh-pee'-nuh") is a request for the production of documents, or a request to appear in court or other legal proceeding.

Voluntary Manslaughter: Voluntary manslaughter is intentionally killing another person in the heat of passion and in response to adequate provocation.

Writ of Habeas Corpus: A *writ of habeas corpus* is a petition filed with the court requesting that a person may be brought before a judge because reasons for their arrest, detention or conviction were in violation of their constitutional rights. The *writ* (pronounced "rit") *of habeas corpus* (pronounced "hay'-bee-uhs korp'-uhs") may also be used as a remedy after their conviction, when any of certain exceptional circumstances has happened (for instance, a person has been deprived of a constitutional right).

ADVANCE REVIEWS

"A compelling, riveting read. I couldn't put it down. This story grabbed me and wouldn't let go. I wanted to know what happened, but I also didn't want it to end. I was inspired by the important history and moved by the powerful story."

Ben Daley,
President
High Tech High Graduate School
of Education

"I'm barely halfway through and I can already see the movie: 'To Kill A Mockingbird meets Selma.' A Black girl and her dog on a journey to meet her best friend's dad in hopes of saving him. All set with the historical background of the civil rights movement and through the point of view of that girl."

John-Arthur Ingram,
Writer and Filmmaker

"Phil Brown, author, delivered a beautiful fictional story filled with diversity, cultures, friendships, children's hopes and dreams, adults living with faith and tragedy. I could not stop reading or put it down and completed reading it in one sitting. This is American history, that as many as possible should have the opportunity to read, share and see on the movie screen. These writings are what I believe are the autobiographies of families that are never told. This is a compelling story of the journey of life through the eyes of children and the importance of family and how life is shaped by war, sacrifice and our thought process and determination to keep oneself moving forward when reality often does not present itself that way... History is powerful."

Diana Love,
Political and Community Activist

"Wow, what a fantastic story. I fell in love with Oli and was completely carried along by the storyline and the strength of Oli's voice. Your ability to weave in the history of the period without the story becoming pedantic and losing its authenticity was really impressive. You retained a hopeful message without it feeling Pollyanna-ish and without white-washing, as it were, the horrific truths of American history. I found the way you ended the story especially powerful—a coalition of like-minded people, fighting on behalf of Oli's dad."

Sheri Bernstein,
Museum Director
Skirball Cultural Center

"I can't get Olivia Jones out of my mind; she reminded me of my childhood growing up in Selma. The 'whites only' signs, not permitted to try on shoes in a store and no explanation from my mom why she drew the outline of my foot onto paper. Olivia's village was filled with love and compassion the same as my village. How I long for the village back for this generation. The writer demonstrated Olivia's passion, energy and determination to help a dear friend. It was filled with suspense and anticipation to the very end, which ended in triumph! This is a must read!"

> **Cynthia Perkins,**
> **First Lady of Selma, Alabama**
> **(Wife of James Perkins, Jr.,**
> **First Black Mayor of Selma**
> **and current Mayor 2020)**

"Thank you for sharing your manuscript as I couldn't put it down and I fell in love with Olivia Jones. Even though it was fictional I just loved the character with the courage and the determination and the desire to realize her dream. All of that courage to actually embark on this journey to find her father and to recreate their family. But there were so many parts to the story and I just loved it! Thank you, Phil, because it was an eye opener to me."

> **Steward Townson**

"Phil Brown balances the views of White southerners

who were conflicted and committed by segregation, as well as the Black people who are the central figures of the manuscript. The book is easily a movie waiting to happen or a three-part miniseries with the ability to take us on a roller coaster ride of human emotions that comes from love, law, patriotism, duty, racism, friendship and all the challenges they create."

Arnold Gordon-Bray, Ret.,
U.S. Army Brigadier General

"Not since the films, *To Kill a Mockingbird* and *Stand by Me*, have I been so moved and compelled (or riveted) by a story about a child's desire to embark upon an adventure to uncover truths that turns into life lessons. Oli's story is gripping and timeless while providing generous moments of levity, reflection and great storytelling."

Christine Swanson,
Director, Writer, Filmmaker

"I've never been someone who likes to read; my mama would tell you this. So when Mr. Phillip asked me to read the *Olivia Jones* manuscript I was really hesitant to say yes—but I finally started reading. I remember stopping to get something to drink and some popcorn. Suddenly I thought, oh shoot, let me get back to the movie I was watching. I opened my computer only to realize that I wasn't watching a movie—I was reading *Olivia Jones!* I was surprised because it felt like I was watching her story—it was that real to me! I just laughed out loud... I love this story!"

Wynter Floyd (18 years old)
Stunt Woman, Cowgirl, College Student

"I read the story about Olivia Jones and was totally captivated by this young lady. Olivia or Oli, as she's called, took me with her on this adventure. I sat listening to Oli and her best friend, Mo, with his other best friend, a German Shepherd named Champ nearby, as they plotted out the plan to journey beyond their little town. The author makes reading Olivia Jones so intimate with rich details that it will draw in the reader, as it did me, to join Oli on her journey in this beautiful story. Olivia Jones is very well crafted and rich with historical events woven throughout so stunningly it prompts the question, is it a true story? It is not."

Jaki Brown,
Hollywood Writer, Producer and three-time Emmy-nominated Prime-time Casting Director

ABOUT THE AUTHOR

Phillip (also known as Phil) A. Brown grew up a second-generation San Diego, California native. Both sets of his grandparents lived within one and a half miles of his childhood home. Phil recalls, "I know now that I lived the quintessential American life. But I also came to know as a young adult that many in my community were not as fortunate. I watched my granddad and dad create businesses that catered to, and employed, members of the community that looked like me. Having mentors and role models in my life shaped who I am and gave me an understanding of 'whose' I am."

For more than four decades Phil has used his gifts, talents and skills to create a positive economic difference in urban underserved communities like the one he grew up in. He focused on creating self-empowerment through historical knowledge of self (Black history), and the power of entrepreneurship and small business development, using cooperative business incubation.

Throughout his journey there's been a central theme—community empowerment. He teaches young African American children about teamwork, self-discipline, confidence and respect through sports such as baseball, tennis and skiing. Through business modeling and scenario simulation, he has been able to transmit his passions for entrepreneurship, community economic development and African American history. These have been the guideposts for his life's work. In 2013, Phil's dad (Jim Brown, who died in November 2020) passed the torch to him and his wife, Lisa, to continue the work of Gateway Educational Foundation (and Institute).

Together they have worked on "Passing the Torch to America's Youth," a tour and series of film documentary projects. This has exposed youth and young adults to Selma, Alabama's rich voting rights history. The tour includes hosting civil rights luminaries in question-and-answer sessions with youth, connecting today's generation to those icons still with us. This important work passes forward the power and significance of civic engagement for social justice through the vote.

The work Phil does today, creating historical fiction such as "Olivia Jones," is another way to center the history of Alabama as an extension of Gateway's work.

ABOUT THE COVER ARTIST

Wendell Wiggins began his education as a visual artist in his hometown, Washington, DC. He attended the Cleveland Institute of Art and pursued his postgraduate studies at the California Institute of the Arts. His career began in Los Angeles. As a graphic designer, illustrator, fine artist, photographer and visual effects director his career spans the film, television, advertising and entertainment arts industries, as well as commissions for murals and private paintings for a wide variety of clients from individuals to companies and businesses. His fine art has been exhibited in galleries and museums throughout the United States and abroad.

ABOUT 1965

Gateway Educational Foundation and Institute has symbolically priced "Olivia Jones" at $19.65 to give honor to the history of Selma, Alabama and the voting rights movement of that year, which ushered in the 1965 Voting Rights Act. Furthermore, a significant portion of the proceeds from each book sale will go toward the preservation and restoration of the Samuel and Amelia Boynton House in Selma and to continue the work of "Passing the Torch to America's Youth."

**PLEASE CONSIDER A GIFT IN HELPING
TO PRESERVE THIS RICH HISTORY!**
Thank you.
ameliaboyntonhouse.com/take-action

CPSIA information can be obtained
at www.ICGtesting.com
Printed in the USA
LVHW112340090522
718365LV00015B/111

9 781088 001868